W9-AYZ-082

SMASHER

SCOTT BLY

THE BLUE SKY PRESS
AN IMPRINT OF SCHOLASTIC INC.
NEW YORK

THE BLUE SKY PRESS

Copyright © 2014 by Scott Bly
All rights reserved.

No part of this publication may be reproduced, stored in a
retrieval system, or transmitted in any form or by any means,
electronic, mechanical, photocopying, recording, or otherwise,
without written permission of the publisher. For information
regarding permission, please write to: Permissions Department,
Scholastic Inc., 557 Broadway, New York, New York 10012.

SCHOLASTIC, THE BLUE SKY PRESS, and associated logos are
trademarks and/or registered trademarks of Scholastic Inc.

Library of Congress catalog card number 2013051217

A note from the author: Although Charlie's story begins in 1542,
I chose to use contemporary language to make the book more
accessible to young readers.

ISBN 978-0-545-14118-5

10 9 8 7 6 5 4 3 2 1   14 15 16 17 18

Printed in the U.S.A.   23
First printing, April 2014

Designed by Jeannine Riske

For Stephen Danger and Michael —
you are both heroes who stare
the unimaginable in the face and
somehow manage to smile

PART I: CHARLIE THE COWARD

CHAPTER 1

A Remote Mountain Hamlet Outside the Village of Eamsford, 1542

■ ■ ■

Tackled by bullies and slammed into mud, Charles couldn't know he would soon encounter far more dangerous enemies. In fact, he would travel through space and time to face a power so terrible it threatened to end civilization. But every tale has a beginning. This one begins with a frog.

"Open yer mouth." Felton Thadwick's heavy knees pinned Charles to the rocky ground.

"No!"

"Open yer mouth. You want yer frog's guts squashed on yer face?"

The smaller boy kept his jaw clenched, his lips tight.

Seamus sneered. "So keep yer mouth closed, yeh prat." He and Rodrick held Charles's wrists and feet.

"Guts on yer face!" Rodrick cheered. All three bullies wanted to see it.

They weren't bluffing. Charles was faster and usually got away. But this time he had slipped on the riverbank.

Felton squeezed Charles's traumatized frog in his meaty fist. Its insides squished. Its eyes bugged out.

Charles couldn't stand it. He closed his eyes and opened his mouth. *At least it isn't a spider.*

Seamus and Rodrick trembled with excitement. Felton stuffed the terrified frog into Charles's mouth, rear end first.

The boy gagged.

"Got somethin' to say in yer stupid accent? Close yer mouth! Careful — yeh'll bite its head off!"

Charles fought the urge to vomit.

Felton pushed on Charles's jaw, squeezing the frog harder. All three Idiot Brothers roared.

"One punch to the chin, Orphan Boy, and it's double pleasure fer me — I get to punch yeh, *and* watch yeh bite the head off a frog." Felton wound up.

Charles braced himself. *I should have left the frog behind. Grandfather will be furious.*

"Hey, Fatty!" A voice yelled before the punch came. Felton froze. He looked up. "Yeah, you, *Fatty*! Why don't you pick on somebody your own size? Oh, *right*! Because there *aren't* any kids your size, you bloated, chicken-bully *loser*!"

Chicken-bully? Loser? The Idiot Brothers peered into the bushes, stunned. That was a *girl's* voice. And it wasn't local.

Charles strained to see. Who dared challenge Felton Thadwick? He tried to wriggle the frog out of his mouth, but Felton jammed it in deeper.

"Where are yeh?" Felton demanded, still peering into the woods. "*Who* are yeh?"

Silence.

Pinned on his back, Charles could only look up. Suddenly, in the tree above, a creature he'd never seen before crept through the branches, camouflaged in the thick leaves. He wanted to scream, but he couldn't because of the frog in his mouth.

Blending into the rough bark, the creature descended the tree with the grace and silence of a panther. As it inched closer, Charles almost choked.

It *was* a girl.

Her mouth moved, but her voice came from a bush off to the left.

"Over here, Fatty!" Felton spun to follow the sound. "No, this way!" Her voice jumped again from a tree to the right, then from a sapling directly ahead.

She crept up behind the Idiot Brothers, throwing her voice to distract them. The leafy pattern on her clothes and skin made her almost invisible, but Charles could still see her raise one finger to her lips to silence him.

"Bullies never change, Fatty." Her accent was unrecognizable. "You're all the same — cowards. *Three* of you ganged up on one kid half your size. But if you had the guts to fight fair, you wouldn't be a bully, would you, *Fatty*?"

Felton was red with rage. "Go *do* something!" he shouted at Seamus and Rodrick. They looked at him uncertainly. Seamus started to run.

Then the mysterious girl struck.

She grabbed Seamus by the neck and yanked him backward, flinging him straight into Rodrick. Both boys crumpled.

Charles squirmed against Felton's grip but still couldn't move. Seamus and Rodrick scrambled up and tried to run, but they weren't fast enough. Seamus yowled as they flew through the air. *Splash!* Straight into the river.

Who *was* she?

Felton was sweating hard. Salty drops spattered Charles's face. The second Felton's grip relaxed, Charles spat out the frog. "Run while you can, Thadwick!"

"Big words," Felton shot back at Charles. "*Yer* the one on the ground."

"Not for long," said the girl. "I'd listen to him, *Fat*wick. Running would be a good idea right now, *coward!*"

Felton bolted.

Charles coughed out the last of the frog slime, then wiped his face. The silence unnerved him. *Am I next?*

A pair of bare brown feet appeared. It took all his courage to look up at her face.

She was unlike anyone he'd ever seen. The leafy pattern that disguised her had changed. Her face was now light brown, like tea with milk. Her long, dark hair was luxurious and thick, and she stepped so lightly she almost seemed to float. The suit she wore was all one piece, and it clung to her body like a second skin. Was she a traveling acrobat?

"My name's Geneva." She held out her hand.

He took it and stood. She was maybe fourteen or fifteen — not much older or bigger than he was. How had she done that?

"Thank you," he said shyly. "I'm Charles."

"Charles, huh?" She grinned. "That's a little formal, don't you think?"

"Formal?" *She's pretty*, he thought, *and exotic*. Her high cheekbones, blue-gray eyes, and tea-colored skin were a sharp contrast to his freckles and sandy brown hair.

"Yeah, Charles. Are you a prince? *Charles* is a name for a king, don't you think? Or an old man."

Well, that was rude!

"No, I'm not a prince. You are not from around here, are you?"

"Nope. You could say I'm visiting. And you know what, Charles? Your fancy name's not gonna work for me. Too stuffy. How about Charlie?"

"*Charlie?* Is that a woman's name?"

"Hardly. Where I'm from, Charlie is a cool boy's name. Something you'd call a good friend. Are you all right?" she asked. "Do they pick on you a lot?"

"Only if they catch me. But I'm fast, and they're big and stupid."

"You're the smart one?"

"I'm very good with puzzles and mathematics."

"I bet that's an understatement," she said with a knowing smile. "I'm guessing you're a genius."

He nodded, unsure of what to say. He didn't talk about his skills. Only his grandfather knew their extent. *Have I said too much? Something is wrong here.* His mouth got dry, and he took a step back.

"And you're good at something else, aren't you?"

Now his face blanched.

"Something secret," she whispered.

"*No!* Puzzles. That's *all.* People like to watch me solve them. If you have heard anything else, it's not true." Her smile no longer seemed friendly.

"Don't worry. I'm not going to tell. But I know about *you.*"

He was silent. *The Hum.* Now he felt it all around them. Could she?

"How's your grandfather?" she asked abruptly.

"What?" His stomach did a backflip. "How do you know about him?"

7

"I've been looking for you, Charlie. It's no accident I found you here."

He swallowed hard. "What do you want?"

"I want to take you somewhere," she said. "Don't you want to see the world, Charlie? Fantastic inventions beyond your wildest dreams?"

"How do you know that?" Charles broke into a sweat. After this morning, he didn't think he could stand one more day with his grandfather. He'd packed to run away. "Who are you?"

"Geneva," she said. "I told you that. I'm not from around here, remember?"

The power of the Hum grew. "Is it you?" he asked quietly.

"No, Charlie. It's you. Your secret is what brought me here."

"There isn't any secret!" This was how they caught you — the Interrogator's spies — they tricked you into talking about it. He would not say a word.

"I need your help, Charlie. In fact, a lot of people do."

"*My* help?"

"I've traveled a long, long way to find you, Charlie. You're very special — and you might be able to save a lot of people. Nobody else can do it. Only you."

"Is this a prank?"

"No! This is real."

"Tell me where you are from," he challenged.

"You won't have heard of it. And you won't believe me."

"Tell me."

"It's not important."

"I am leaving." Charles took a step back.

"Stop!"

"Tell me."

She sighed. "I'm from a city called LAanges."

"Lahn-what?"

"I told you it was a place you wouldn't know."

"Where is it?"

"Far away. LAanges. In another language it means 'angels.' I said you wouldn't believe me."

"Are you an angel?"

She laughed. "No! I'm just from a city a long way from now." Then she became serious again. Urgent. "I need to take you there. Everything depends on it. Please help."

"What if I don't want to go?"

"But you do. I can see it in your eyes. And you want to know more, don't you? Admit it."

He didn't move. He felt dizzy.

"I promise you won't be sorry. Meet me here tomorrow at dawn. Be ready to travel."

"Where do you want me to go?"

"To LAanges — a world that could fall apart unless you help. See you at sunrise, Charlie. Terrible things might happen if you don't go. Unspeakable things. Everything depends on you. Everything."

"What if I don't want to go?" he asked again.

She didn't answer. Her clothes shifted back to camouflage, blending into the brush behind her.

"Wait!" Charles cried.

Crack! A flash of light lit the woods, accompanied by a deep rumble and a wet, slushy rattle. Geneva had completely disappeared. His stomach flipped again.

The Hum. It had to be. Why else would a stranger come from a foreign place to find me? He shivered. *My father. My grandmother. My mother. Am I next?* Hundreds of his kind had been hunted down, tortured, and put to death. Of course he was afraid.

"Geneva . . ." He said it under his breath.

Her words echoed in his mind.

I've been looking for you, Charlie. . . . Looking for you . . . It's no accident . . .

CHAPTER 2

The City of LAanges, 2042

∎∎∎

"Mr. Foxx? Your evening appointment is here." Evelyn Rasmussin's voice chimed over the expensive VisaFon on Gramercy Foxx's vast mahogany desk. The phone's camera revealed only the back of Foxx's leather chair. He spoke without kindness.

"Send him in. Then go home, Evelyn."

"Yes, Mr. Foxx." Uncertainty crossed her face as the screen blanked. The camera on his end was rarely on. She could never tell if he was watching or not, so she kept her smile in place during video calls, even after regular work hours. Better safe than sorry.

She was relieved she could leave. Having worked for Foxx for more than five years, Evelyn should have felt comfortable with her boss. But the business he conducted after hours left her uneasy.

Almost as unsettling was the man's face. He slept in the private office and residence on the 199th floor, assuming he slept at all. But his face . . . It never showed any sign of exhaustion. She knew that some nights he worked until dawn without sleep. Yet Foxx always appeared fresh and rested. It gave her a creepy feeling.

Foxx spent more time at the office and less time in public than any other CEO Evelyn had encountered. She didn't think he had set foot outside the new TerraThinc Building since they moved in a year ago.

"You're late, Lawrence," Foxx snapped when the towering double doors to his office swung open. The skinny young man with pocked skin pushed his glasses up, grateful that Foxx's back was still turned.

He wasn't the only one.

A shadowy figure, clinging to the corner ceiling above a potted plant, blended into the leaves. It waited. And watched.

Lawrence Yates was taken aback by the view. From the 200th floor, the night lights of LAanges stretched far into the distance, twinkling through the haze below. He made out three or four wildly expensive and largely illegal Sky Cars, Foxx's newest craze. The flying dots crisscrossed above the traffic-clogged freeways.

Foxx ruled his empire from the top of one of the tallest and most technologically advanced skyscrapers in the world. He had built the TerraThinc Building to house the headquarters of his corporation of the same name. The thin haze blanketing the city was a remnant from decades of smog. TerraThinc had been instrumental in much of the terraforming of the last ten years, which had stopped the onset of climate change caused by global warming. The cleanup hadn't saved the ice caps, but visibility had increased by miles.

But Foxx didn't appreciate the view. He *expected* it. His TerraThinc Building was the newest mega-skyscraper among those being built by the super-wealthy. The recent economic collapse had only strengthened his dominance over his corporate competitors. The view went with the territory.

"Mr. Foxx, I told you I don't meet with clients. I made it clear we would only work over the web. This had better be important." Lawrence Yates was talking to the back of the leather chair. He had promised himself he would take a strong first step. He didn't allow other rich clients to push him around. Why should he let Foxx? "For you to insist on meeting with me to review this virus is so far out of line that —"

"*Silence,*" Foxx commanded, his back still turned. "You write computer viruses — good ones. They will grow even better under my direction. But that is *all* you do. *I* make the decisions. *I* determine the strategy. *I* move the pieces. Is that clear?"

Yates nervously bit the inside of his cheek. His throat made a clicking sound — a nervous tic that came out under stress. Yates stood to make more in the next month than he had in five years.

"Yes, we're clear," Yates said, barely hiding his resentment.

"Good. I see you have delicate hands. My last programmer lost the use of his fingers. He was so accident prone. Isn't that sad? Show me our creation."

A trio of shimmering AquaFase immersive screens across from Foxx's desk entered phase-change. Yates's attempt to be strong with Foxx had fallen flat. Now the pressure was on. *Click click.*

"I brought the code," Yates said quietly. His hand trembled, jingling the magnets of his Data Bone bracelet. He brought it close enough to pull the data. A chair creaked. Foxx must have finally turned to face him. Yates was too frightened to look over his shoulder. His program displayed on the AquaFase plasmice screen.

"My worm can penetrate most corporate firewalls, and it can launch from any web browser." *Click click.* "It works like your garden-variety email viruses, too, launching as an attachment. And it root-kits under the OS — *any* OS — even the lightweight net stuff. But the best part is that it can exploit router and switch firmware, converting one form of traffic to another. It can dodge pretty much all forms of antivirus and anti —"

"Yes, of course," Foxx interrupted dismissively. "Lawrence, I'd like to show you some of *my* work tonight. One programmer to another."

"You're a programmer, too?" Before Yates realized what he was doing, he turned to look at Foxx. His stomach dropped when he saw the man's face.

Gramercy Foxx had appeared in every form of media for more than a decade. Before he had gone into seclusion, he had appeared in 3D-casts and even some of the new hologram shows he had pioneered. But the camera, even with the triple-lens 3D, did not capture the inhumanity within his taut and timeless face.

He looked as if he could be in his forties. But something intangible suggested he was far older — fifty, sixty, eighty — it was impossible to tell. His face was perfectly preserved, and it lacked the stretched look of plastic surgery. Yates sensed that Foxx's pale blue eyes had seen countless years, though they revealed nothing. The only other signs of age were the silver streaks at his temples in his slicked-back, deep brown hair.

"I dabble," Foxx replied, baring his teeth in a smile that seemed far too carnivorous for comfort. Yates turned back to the monitors. *Click click.*

At a wave of Foxx's hand, lasers illuminated the water-based screens. Yates's program disappeared, replaced by new lines of code. On another screen, shapes and objects flowed in and out like moving architectural art. This programming technique was far more intuitive and efficient than reading lines of code.

Yates followed the endless stream of data, amazed. "I've never seen anything like this. It could take control of a computer, even networking gear. The artificial intelligence is extraordinary! It's avoiding detection here, and sabotaging the . . ."

Yates touched the screen, actually sticking his hands *into* it, pausing the scroll of code. He inspected programming objects by grabbing and twisting them.

Yates lingered over a complex spiral, struggling to comprehend it. "How did you ever think of this?"

"Beginner's luck," Foxx said with false modesty.

"How would you actually use this?"

"It's a hybrid — part standard computer virus, part biological virus. We have a lot to learn from nature." Foxx let his words sink in. "Lawrence, I'd like to blend my code with yours. We'll spread this virus together."

"I work *alone*, Mr. Foxx. The biggest software developer in the world tried to hire me three times. I turned him down. But . . . if we *did* blend code, what computers do you want to control with this?" He pulled his hands away, and couldn't resist bragging. "I spread the Nonsense virus to thirty million systems in six hours last fall."

"I know all about the Nonsense virus, Lawrence. You cost my IT department seven hundred thousand in the first hour alone. No hard feelings, of course." He flashed his famous smile. "This isn't just for computers. Have another look, my boy. Don't tell me you can't spot it. A coder as advanced as you are can easily identify the fumblings of a novice like me, right?"

Yates was piqued. *No one* doubted his Kung Fu. His vision filled with the hypnotic surge of moving shapes and code.

Foxx waved his hand again. The AquaFase flashed faster and faster, pulsing in rhythms not yet apparent.

Was Foxx singing? Yates was imagining things. *Click click.*

"This goes far beyond controlling computers, Lawrence. With this virus, I plan to control more — much more. And you will have the honor of being the first. . . ."

Foxx rose from his chair. He locked his arms in a tense semicircle above Yates. The programmer's body jolted and stiffened. Foxx's hands danced in a disjointed rhythm with the patterns flashing on-screen. He was a master puppeteer above his marionette. Yates twitched into unnatural positions, seemingly at Foxx's command.

Then, as suddenly as it began, it stopped. Foxx collapsed in his chair, his face drained. The young man froze at the screen, silent. His body was tense but no longer contorted.

Foxx took a deep, shuddering breath and pulled himself upright. "Who is your master?" he rasped.

No response.

Foxx asked again, more forcefully, "Who is your master?"

"My master's name . . . is Callis. He alone . . . commands me. You are . . . Callis?"

"Yes, I am Callis," Foxx said. "Go. Your lab is ready. You know what to do."

Yates rose with unnatural fluidity. He took a plastic card from Foxx's hand and did not look back as he left.

Gramercy Foxx slumped down into his chair again. A smile of utter contentment crossed his face. He closed his eyes to rest. What a satisfying first move in his glorious chess game against humanity.

Across the office, opposite the conference table, the upper leaves of a potted bamboo palm rustled and quietly exhaled. Camouflage rendered the spy nearly invisible. Watching Foxx's closed eyelids and steady breathing, the intruder carefully descended, clinging gecko-like to the wall.

Padding silently to the door, Geneva looked back over her shoulder at Foxx. She shuddered. His experiments had progressed beyond anything she could have imagined.

Callis. She'd been receiving cryptic messages in the back of her mind for months. There had been signs, but now she'd seen the undeniable truth with her own eyes.

She needed to keep moving. Charlie was expecting her — *if* he decided to come back with her to LAanges. In three hours, it would be dawn in Eamsford. *Three hours minus five hundred years*, she corrected herself. She hoped he was brave. He would have to be.

CHAPTER 3

Charles couldn't sleep. He hadn't told his grandfather about the girl. Now, restless and irritable, he stared at the cracked ceiling and went over the day's events.

First Grandfather refused to accept Charles's hard work, *again.* "Repeat!" Grandfather snapped with a whack to the hands. Charles would run away soon. This time he meant it. Then Felton had caught him with the frog. And Geneva . . .

She didn't act like someone trying to hunt him down, but how could he be sure? His grandfather always warned him: Do not trust anyone — even people you know.

They had been hiding out in these mountains as long as Charles could remember. So much of what he saw and did stayed behind locked doors. How could Geneva know about his grandfather? Did she know about the murders? But if she wanted to hurt him, why had she saved him from the Idiot Brothers?

Geneva spoke of a city named after angels. No, he did not think she would turn him in. Exhausted by unanswered questions, he finally drifted off.

Suddenly he woke with a start. The sun would be rising soon. *The old man thinks that by being nasty to me, he can wash all that blood off his hands. Well, he can't.* Charles would take his chances and go.

He took one last look around the bare room. What made him hesitate? Grandfather? No, Grandfather was impossible to please. Charles had known for a long time that the only way to stop the old man was to leave.

His three tutors said Charles was a mathematical genius, a prodigy. They said he was a born master — the Hum roared through him. He would become legendary. But every accomplishment brought only one thing — another smack with the cane.

Day after day Grandfather barked at Charles, snapping instructions. "Your mother did that when she was *two* years old! Attend to your lessons and not on how talented you think you are! You must prepare! Remember the prophecy: A time will come when the Hum will no longer serve us — no one will *feel* it, or even *believe* in it. If the law is passed, we'll all be hanged. Study, boy! You're the new generation. Study to keep it *alive.*"

Well, I'm not going to study anymore, Charles thought stubbornly. *I don't care about the prophecy. I don't have a single friend. I'm not even allowed to have a dog!*

On his school slate, he scratched a simple good-bye message:

I HAVE GONE TO SEE THE ANGELS. I WILL PRACTICE EVERY DAY.

There. Let Grandfather figure *that* out.

Charles made his way down to the river. The sun was beginning to rise. A bird flew overhead, and a blue feather fell to the ground. Charles picked it up and put it in his pocket. Maybe it would be good luck.

Splash! The girl's laughter rippled out of the water, but she wasn't there.

"You *do* want to come," a voice said.

"I . . . I do," he stammered into the air.

"So ask me a question, Charlie!"

"Where are you *from*?"

"*LAanges.* I told you that. Ask another!"

"Come out where I can see you."

"I'm right in front of your face!" The bushes parted. Her camouflage was perfect. "The question to ask is not *where* am I from, but *when*. *When* am I from, Charlie?"

She stepped in front of an oak, and her colors immediately blended to match the tree trunk. "I'm from five hundred years in your future, and halfway around the world." She cocked her head and waited for his reaction.

"You're insane!"

"I'm very sane and very serious. I came from the future to ask for your help."

"Don't be ridiculous."

"I came because you can do things no one else can do — from any place or any time. You have a gift. It's in your blood."

A gift. A terrible, frightful gift that makes it impossible to trust anyone. If she's lying, I'll end up dead like my father, my mother, my grandmother — who never hurt a living thing, not even a spider.

The thought made him sick. "Go back where you came from!" He started to run.

A sharp, piercing wail shattered the silence of the woods. Its vibration made his teeth ache, and he covered his ears with his hands. Just when he thought his head would explode, the siren stopped.

"I can do that again!" Geneva called after him. "Every person in your village will have heard me, Charlie. If they aren't already on their way, then I bet Fatwick will lead them straight here. And who are they going to find? Not me. I'll disappear. Then they'll remember the rumors about your grandmother."

"Do not speak of her!" he shouted.

"Then come with me, Charlie. I'm begging you! Please! Help me!"

"Help you what?" he said, fighting to control his anger.

"Stop a terrible man from enslaving the world — everyone! I'm telling the truth. I am from the future. Let me show you the way," she said. "It's over here. You'll see."

She ran to the riverbank and waded in, knee-deep. Arms in a wide circle, she brought the tips of her pointer fingers close together, her thumbs straight up. She frowned and squeezed her eyes shut, deep in concentration.

"Can you feel it?" she whispered.

He could. His skin tingled. It was the Hum, even more intense than yesterday.

"Come on, atoms," she said hoarsely. "Smash!" She touched her fingers together.

Flash! A bright light burst from Geneva's fingertips. "Smasher!" The air popped with a wet hiss. She pinched her fingers together over the light — grabbing it, pulling it. She

21

twisted and spread her arms high and low. The point of light grew into a bright disk.

Then she released it. A shimmering pool of watery blue light hovered a few inches above the surface of the river like a window.

"Do you believe me now?"

"What *is* it?"

"It's a void, Charlie. That's how I got here. And that's how we're going to LAanges. It's a Resonant Gap in the geometry and frequency of the universe. The laws of physics — the rules that hold the world together — they can be . . . *bent* a little. Or stretched. I can open a gap and jump in! On the other side, we're beyond space and time. When we jump back out, we'll be somewhere else, or some *time* else."

"How do I know you're telling the truth?"

"Just look at that thing!" she snapped, exasperated. "Have a little faith, Charlie. And you can always come back."

"You promise I can come back?"

"I *promise*. Will you go?"

"Yes."

Without another word, she jumped into the vertical pool with a sideways splash.

"Wait!"

But it was too late. The bottoms of her feet kicked off and disappeared.

Was it water? He poked it. It moved like water, except it hung in midair and rippled sideways. And his finger was dry. Smasher had to be connected to the Hum — everything was.

Where had she gone?

Have a little faith. He wanted to go. He'd said he would go. But now he was paralyzed with fear.

The sound of voices startled him, reminding him of the danger in his own village. People had heard the loud noise and were coming. He looked at the impossible, glowing fluid. They would see this. They would think it was him — the Hum. Their suspicion and fear would whip them into a frenzy.

Smash through time?

Charles peered into the swirling vortex.

And he leaped.

CHAPTER 4

Charles was submerged, but it wasn't exactly water. Was he under time — or space? He was surrounded by a blue glow.

Countless points of light stretched into the distance. They reminded him of stars.

A voice from a thousand miles away floated to his ears.

Charlie. It was Geneva. *Charlie! Focus!*

Suddenly she appeared. Her lips didn't move, but Charles could hear her. *Focus! Right here!* She yanked his arm so hard it hurt. Then she pulled him. The speed was almost incomprehensible.

One of the points of light grew larger. It expanded to the size of a window. Geneva pushed it with all her strength, and then — *clank* — she sailed through, hauling Charles behind her.

"*Oof!*" He slammed down onto solid ground. Another yank. Geneva pushed him against a stone wall.

"Where are we?"

"LAanges. More than five hundred years in the future!"

He squinted into blaring sunlight. The sights, smells, and sensations of traveling to a huge city in the future were too overwhelming. He felt dizzy.

"Snap out of it," Geneva said. "We have to go see Gramercy Foxx."

"Who is that?"

"He's the reason you came here." She reached behind a Dumpster where she'd stashed a tattered blue jacket. "Put this on. You need to fit in. Come on."

As she led him down the alley, her black one-piece outfit shimmered, shuddered, and shook itself out. The fabric shrank, stretched, and rewove itself into a loose lavender shirt and baggy white pants.

Charles blinked. "How do you do that?"

"It's advanced nano-web fabric, mostly made of carbon nanotubes and self-assembling magnetic relays."

"What?"

"I'll explain it later."

"No shoes?"

"Too confining. Can't feel the ground. Come on, this way."

They were walking fast through crowds of strange people in even stranger clothes. Charles didn't feel a glimmer of the Hum. *Is this the future Grandfather described? Where people can't sense it?*

"How did you connect to the Hum through that Smasher thing you did?" Charles asked.

"What do you mean? I didn't connect to anyone."

"Yes you did. You used the Hum to travel through time. How did you do it?"

"The Hum? Is that what you call it? Cool! I want to hear about it — everything you know. We don't have it here. At least nobody does but Gramercy Foxx . . . and now *you*."

"Why not?"

Geneva didn't answer. She was almost running.

"Where are we going?"

"To see Gramercy Foxx. We're almost there. You need to keep up, Charlie. I'll explain it later."

Charlie, he thought. *Something you'd call a good friend.* He was starting to like it.

Now she stopped and pointed up. They stood in front of the tallest skyscraper in the city.

"This is the TerraThinc Building," Geneva said. "Follow me, and keep your head down. If they catch us, it'll be bad."

"Catch us?"

Whoosh! Geneva had already rotated out of view behind revolving doors.

Charles followed. Every aspect of LAanges — and the future — was astonishing and mesmerizing. The lobby of TerraThinc was jammed with people talking, but not to each other. "Geneva," he asked, "what are they doing?"

"Notice they're all wearing glasses? Those are displays. They're having HoloChats."

"Hollow-*what?*"

"Hologram Chats. They're talking to their friends."

She pulled him to a set of doors marked "Observation Deck Elevators" that slid open, and Geneva pushed him in with a mob of tourists. She squeezed his hand, and the elevator took off.

Charlie. It is a good name for a friend.

Up. They were going up and up and up. His ears popped. Seconds later, they stepped out onto a viewing platform. The sharp wind and staggering size of the sprawling city left him breathless.

He was weak in the knees when Geneva pulled him away to a small door. She punched a few buttons, and a second door clicked open. Then she led him up a flight of stairs.

"Where are we going?"

"To the very top."

He peered down over the stairwell railing. The sight of the bottomless spiral made him queasy. Seven flights up, they reached a sign that read "Roof Access — Authorized Personnel Only." Geneva stopped at the security panel and pressed more numbers. The door clicked open. Charles looked at her in amazement.

"Technology, Charlie. Pretty soon you'll know all about it. No different than the wheel or the horseshoe." She held the door open for him. "After you."

A huge rush of wind almost knocked Charles off his feet.

"Hey! Come over here, to the edge. Look at my ladder."

"I don't see any ladder. Is this one of your Smasher things?"

"No." She made him feel along the edge of the roof with his fingertips. "Can you *feel* it? Look again. Right . . . there!"

A black ladder suddenly became visible to Charles. It descended down, down, down. When he moved an inch, it vanished. "Wow!"

"Negative refraction," Geneva explained. "I call it Cloaking. It's one of the ways I spy on him."

"Who?"

"Gramercy Foxx! The terrible man! The reason you're here. This is *his* building. That ladder hangs right outside his office."

"You want *me* to spy on him? Why?"

She pointed at the ladder. "You climb down that, and then you look at him through his office window. I'm pretty sure what he's doing is connected to your gift. I think he has it, too. If I'm right, you'll sense it."

The Hum again. Had Grandfather been right?

"Aren't there any people like me anymore?" he asked softly.

"No, Charlie. Except maybe Foxx, and if he has your power . . ." She let out a deep sigh. "Well, you need to find out."

Slowly Charles climbed over the ledge and onto the ladder. Step by step, he descended. *Do not look down.*

Above him, Geneva smiled. She had been right about Charlie. Time was running out, but at least they had a chance. There was so much to tell the human. She would wait for the right moment to let him know the truth.

CHAPTER 5

Gramercy Foxx had no difficulty attracting all twelve of the most influential businesspeople in the world for his meeting. They stood, transfixed by the codes and images on the wall-size displays.

"I'm so glad you could be here to share this moment." Foxx spoke from behind. "I've chosen to call my newest offering 'The Future.' I want to share it first with you, my most trusted associates — the inner circle. As always, you are sworn to secrecy."

"We knew you were working on something big, Foxx, but this is amazing!" James Cricket, CEO of Global Oil, shook his head. "That is, if it really does what you suggest. How can a *product* truly provide serenity and peace of mind?"

"You doubted his hologram devices, though, didn't you, James? And they worked out." Terrence Wrightwood was the leader of early cloud and solarium Internet systems. Now ninety-seven, he needed an oxygen cell to breathe. "Gramercy, I'm sure it will be your finest work yet."

"I agree, and *Time Man* is my favorite 3D show." Janice Wong beamed at Foxx. "The Future will accomplish more for society than the automobile! This makes InterNext look simplistic." Janice Wong wrote the code that brought InterNext connectivity to every piece of electrical equipment imaginable. In one move, you could update your calendar, set the alarm clock, program a Smart Coffeepot, and adjust your Smart Lights to dim for bedtime. "We'll have to prepare for this, Foxx. Change of this nature must be *evolutionary*, not *revolutionary*."

"You'll have time," Foxx assured them, "while the TerraThinc marketing machine gets rolling."

"We'll need to get our products ready to compete with yours!" Dick Crawford joked. Crawford's orbiting weapons systems could vaporize a single person or an entire city block anywhere in the world — in less than a minute. "When will you reveal it?"

"I will announce the date tomorrow."

"No! We have to know *now*, Gramercy," Tom Dennis said. He was the man who engineered the deregulation of banks and mergers that had led to a worldwide economic collapse. Everyone in the room had raked in record profits.

"Come now," Foxx cooed, almost musically. "Isn't it enough to be the first to see my technology? And I do promise it will change the world as we know it."

"You gained your success with our collective blessing." The warmth was gone from Wrightwood's voice.

"Let's not bicker over details." Foxx ignored Wrightwood's threat.

"We opened the door for you," Crawford growled. "Tom's right. We need to know more *now*. Don't even think about crossing us."

Foxx suppressed a smile. He was about to cross all of them.

"Friends! Enough bickering! You haven't seen the best part. How about a sample? Prepare to become more relaxed than you have ever been before. Watch the screens, watch the screens."

All twelve men and women turned to view the last images their free minds would ever see.

Two hundred stories above ground, Charles was watching. His hand slipped, and he struggled to pull himself up. *How did I end up here? I'm no hero!* The wind made his eyes burn.

The people and the screens' images were not what caught Charles's attention, however. He was relieved to feel the familiar — and surprisingly strong — tingle of the Hum. So powerful here! He hadn't felt a trace of it anywhere else. He could even see its telltale glow, though no one else would. Geneva was right about Gramercy Foxx.

Foxx's guests didn't hear him softly begin his fragile chant to tap into the deep, endless power of the Hum. They didn't see his hands dancing to the peculiar rhythms.

The wall of screens flashed, but Foxx had refined his technique since he'd tested it on Yates; his confidence had grown. Now his plan would progress to its next crucial step.

Six minutes passed, and he was finished.

Outside, on the ladder, Charles sat perfectly still.

The room fell silent. The screens dimmed. In a hushed yet commanding voice, Foxx asked, "Who is your master?"

The twelve answered in perfect unison. "Our master is Callis. You are our master."

"I am." Foxx leered at the eldest. "Wrightwood, come."

Terrence Wrightwood stood stiffly. His knees wobbled. He took a few unsteady steps. His eyes were lifeless.

"Terrence Wrightwood, who is your master?" Foxx demanded.

"My master is Callis. You are my master."

"And you will obey my command."

"Yes."

"Terrence Wrightwood, you will fall into a coma. You are to never wake up. You will not die now. You will live an unnaturally long life. You will die only when I allow it. You will wait forever if I choose."

"As you command."

"Do it now."

Perched on the invisible ladder, Charles watched a terrible glow pour out of Foxx.

The brittle, old man collapsed.

The strength of the Hum was unmistakable. Every bone in Charles's body tingled.

Gramercy Foxx came over to the window. He gazed out. Something was amiss. A strange flicker interrupted the flow of his power. What was it? His past, resurfacing to haunt him?

No. He refused to allow unpleasant memories to spoil his satisfaction. Not tonight.

He smiled, contemplating his next move as he turned back to his guests. The virus had been a success. Everything was in place.

Foxx had been inches away from Charles, but Geneva's invisible ladder worked perfectly. A twisted, corrupted abomination of the Hum was coursing through the ageless man. The encounter was making Charles sick. First, his hands went numb, and then . . .

Slam! Charles's foot slipped through the rungs. His knee knocked into the glass window of Foxx's office.

Gramercy Foxx spun at the sound. *What was that thump?*

He looked at the window but saw nothing unusual. *Another stupid bird, slamming into the glass.* He turned abruptly and returned to his guests.

None of the other eleven leaders of industry had blinked an eye when Terrence Wrightwood fell to the floor.

"Who is your master?" Foxx asked again.

"Our master is Callis. You are our master."

"Now you will return to consciousness and help Mr. Wrightwood." Foxx raised his hands.

Clap!

"Wrightwood!" the others shouted, and rushed to him.

Foxx pressed the intercom on his desk.

"Evelyn, call an ambulance! There's been an accident!" His voice sounded urgent, almost as if he cared.

Charles, nearly hypnotized by Foxx, was losing consciousness. Fast as lightning, Geneva darted down the ladder. She flipped her feet toward the sky and caught him, defying gravity as casually as if she were standing right-side up on solid ground. The skin of her fingers and toes rippled into millions of microscopic hooks, each entangling the electrical fields of the molecules of Charles's skin and the ladder.

Charles shook off the numb feeling. "How did you do that? You moved so fast!"

"Gecko mode. But forget about me. What did you see?" She lifted Charles up onto the roof.

"You were right. It was the Hum!" he choked out. "I could feel it!"

The sickness in the pit of his stomach hit him again. "I . . . I . . . I think I *recognize* him. But from where?"

CHAPTER 6

When Charles woke up the next morning, he was in a small, dingy room on the 2nd floor of an abandoned building. He was lying on a couch, but he did not remember how he got there.

Now he looked curiously around the small room.

"Someone sealed this place up years ago," Geneva told him. "They forgot about the dumbwaiter to the alley. It's a secret way to get in and out. You were so tired last night I carried you all the way here. We're a couple of miles from the TerraThinc Building. This is my hideout." She touched a screen, and a news report flashed on. "See, we're streaming media. . . ."

On the screen, a woman spoke beside a crush of people. "We're live from City Hospital, where Gramercy Foxx's emergency press conference is under way. Mr. Foxx has announced his new creation: 'The Future.'"

"Who is *she*?" Charles asked.

"Jane Virtue. She's the only honest reporter in town. Shhhhh."

Gramercy Foxx addressed a throng of men and women from the press. "My dear friend Terrence Wrightwood believed The Future would bring us all together. Help me make his dream come true. In twenty days, I will release The Future to everyone, everywhere. Imagine finally having peace of mind! And I promise the world will never, ever be the same."

Geneva turned off the news feed, disgusted. *"Twenty days,"* she said. "Twenty days to figure out how to stop him."

"Last night he hypnotized all those people. Is that The Future he's talking about?"

"It has to be. He's marketing it as if it can make your life perfect! But he's taking away free will. When people look into a computer screen, the system infects them like a virus."

"Does everyone look into computer screens?"

"Yes! Everybody!" Geneva snapped. Then she caught herself. "Right. This is all new to you. I'm sorry. Computers are everywhere — phones, TVs, on toilets! Computers can catch viruses — sicknesses — but until now, a computer can't make a *person* sick. That's the creepiest thing about it, Charlie. Somehow he's mixing a computer virus with a biological virus so a person can catch it from a computer, or from another person. It's going to spread like wildfire."

"Will it spread from the old people who got it last night?"

"I don't think so. He doesn't seem to be finished yet. He's adding the infectious part to the final code."

"How do you know?"

"Because I've been spying on him."

"Aren't other people spying on him, too?"

"I can spy on him in ways nobody else can. I have abilities — my sight, my hearing, my technology — that are beyond human."

"What does that mean?"

"I wanted to wait to tell you, but you need to know now."

"Tell me what?"

"About who I am. I look like a girl, but I'm not human, Charlie. I have human parts, but I'm a robot."

"What is a *robot*?"

"I wasn't *born*, I was *built*. I'm a machine — an advanced synthesis of biotech, nanotech, computer tech, and nuclear energy!" A strange light suddenly beamed from her eyes onto her palms. The skin of her hands vibrated, and the light reflected into the air above, creating moving holographic images that danced overhead.

"Wow! How do you do that? Can you teach me?"

"No. You'd have to be made of plasmonic processors, holographic storage, a particle accelerator, cyberhydronetics . . . things like that. I'm a *robot*." Then her eyes went dark. "I've never told anyone before."

Charles sat quietly for a moment and stared at her, completely confused. "What's a robot?" he asked again. "You *are* some kind of angel, aren't you?"

"Angel? No! I'm an *invention*! No different than a table or a carriage. I'm made of more metal than flesh and blood. Robots were invented to help people. I'm a machine that follows directions. I only *seem* human."

She looked away. Was she ashamed? "You're . . . an *invention*? An invention that looks like a real girl?"

Had that been a flicker of pain Charles had seen in her eyes?

"I didn't want to tell you yet," Geneva said. "What do I know about things like the Hum, or friendship, or happiness? I'm just a machine pretending to be a real person."

She hates herself, Charlie thought. But she made it sound as if robots didn't have feelings. He still didn't understand what a robot was, but he knew Geneva was no normal girl. *She's better*, he thought. *She can do much more than I can. And what defined being a human, anyway? Who cares if she's made of metal? She's tough, but she's kind. She does have feelings. And she's trying to save the world!*

Geneva wouldn't look at him. She played with her fingers, flexing her skin into different shapes and textures.

Charlie — something you'd call a good friend, she had said. "You know," he told her softly, "I think you're amazing. Look at what you've done! And look at what you're doing! If you're a robot, then that's what I want to be."

"No you don't."

"I do."

"Then you don't know what you're talking about."

She finally looked at him. He could see the faint beginning of a smile. "Thanks, Charlie."

"I decided you can call me that."

"Whatever," she said with a grin. "Watch this, Charlie." Then she rolled her eye beams around in different directions and made a light show on the ceiling.

"And you should know, it's not *math* I love — it's solving *puzzles*."

"Perfect. Because Gramercy Foxx has given us quite a puzzle to solve."

CHAPTER 7

Gramercy Foxx had set an unstoppable machine into motion. A wild frenzy erupted across the globe. Every form of international media frantically guessed what The Future might be. Every crackpot inventor developed a spin-off of The Future . . . and no one even knew what it was.

Foxx was ecstatic. Humans were driven to consume, and they followed directions. Especially the trendsetters in LAanges. Even after the worldwide economic collapse, they continued to set the pace for the rest of the planet. Other countries despised their excess and greed, but people all over the globe still hungered for more, more, more.

Stuff. They wanted more stuff.

For years Foxx had been ratcheting up the public's need to have ever-increasing collections of products. He had diverted the public's attention from truly important events and slowly turned news into entertainment. Money poured in. Eventually even entertainment news was pushed out by worse and worse mindless dreck. Foxx hadn't come up with the idea. He'd just perfected it.

Now the same techniques were selling The Future. Drive them crazy with desire, and they would stampede to the feeding troughs.

Let them come.

Over the next six days, Foxx made calls, sent emails, and deployed automated software that wrote blog postings under pseudonyms. The Future was coming, and it was the biggest thing ever released in the world. With no idea what it might be, people read everything and watched everything — all for a glimpse of what The Future might hold.

Through it all, Foxx kept every shred of it a secret. Some publications received "exclusive" information that The Future was a new generation of flying vehicles powered by hydrogen to eliminate traffic and pollution forever. Others learned from "a source close to Foxx" that The Future was a brain chip implant for pleasure and prosperity. And still others heard "off the record" that The Future was an energy source more abundant than water. Foxx's personal favorite was when one of Foxx's "top advisers" leaked that it was a time machine. Oh, the irony.

It all added up to a perfect storm of blitz advertising. *And just wait until the real marketing campaign begins.*

CHAPTER 8

Meanwhile, at the hideout, Geneva gave Charlie a crash education on computers, science, and technology. She lectured tirelessly, hour after hour. Fortunately, Charlie was a sponge. She had never seen anyone learn so fast.

"OK, trivia time. Did you know that very early mathematicians used a counting board to —"

"I know all about that," Charlie interrupted. He was tired, but math came easily. "I use an abacus for calculations. It's fun. Did *you* know that some say the abacus was invented by the Babylonians, not the Chinese?"

"Sure, and the abacus led to the invention of the calculator and eventually the computer . . . but remember, we're talking about language."

"Do you know why numbers go to ten?" Charlie challenged. He was sure he would stump her with this one.

Geneva held up her hands, fingers spread wide.

"Ten fingers!" Charlie laughed. "You know *everything*!"

"*Most* civilizations counted to ten," she corrected. "That's called a base-ten number system — because each digit has ten possible numbers before you add another digit. But the Babylonians — they used a number system based on *sixty*."

"Like your clock!"

"*Exactly*. The Babylonians *developed* timekeeping. Sixty seconds to a minute, sixty minutes to an hour."

"Oooh, base-sixty, then, right?"

"Yeah. But let's bring it back to Foxx. His code is numbers, and computers speak in numbers. Computers speak in a base-two number system called binary."

"Which is why you gave me this binary abacus. . . ."

"Correct. You have to learn the language. Math is a language of numbers."

Charlie had never thought of math as a *language*. He liked the puzzles his grandfather gave him — number puzzles, logic puzzles, word puzzles, *any* puzzles. He would stay up all night to finish one. "You'll need mathematics to survive in the world if the prophecy is true," Grandfather always said. *Blah, blah, blah.* "One day, the Hum will disconnect, and the world will —"

Charlie stopped cold. *The prophecy. The Hum will disconnect.* Something about a leader and the whole world. And, and . . .

He couldn't remember. A thunderstorm pounded outside. He listened to the rain and amped up his mind, trying to recall.

After all the times he had heard it, now when he needed it, the story was gone. *Poof.*

Geneva interrupted his thoughts. "I'm running low on power," she said.

"What?"

"It's going to take a while for my ultra-capacitors to recharge. There isn't enough voltage from my long-term storage to charge them."

"Voltage — that's electrical . . . *pressure*, right?"

"Bingo. Like water pressure."

"Electromagnetism is one of the three fundamental forces of nature."

"Yeah, but it's called the electro-weak force, actually," Geneva corrected. "Gravity and the strong nuclear force are the other two. Right now, I need to find some lightning."

"And lightning is a form of static electricity. Why do you need lightning?"

"To recharge. You stay here and get some rest. You're going to need it."

"I won't be able to sleep." He didn't want to tell her about the prophecy, but he couldn't stop thinking about it.

"Well, then practice your binary math on the abacus. Remember, ones and zeroes. And stay *hidden*," Geneva stressed. "I'll be gone a while." She climbed into the dumb-waiter and stepped out into the rain.

Charlie tried to remember the details of the prophecy. The Hum might fade . . . but the Hum was the life energy that composed the whole world and everything beyond it. How could the world continue to exist if the Hum faded away? Or maybe the Hum was still here, but humans had disconnected to it. They had stopped believing.

Was it possible Geneva lived in a world that denied the existence of the Hum? Only Gramercy Foxx still seemed to hold the connection. . . .

Gaaazzzzaaap! Geneva's metal fingertip attracted the lightning bolt exactly as she planned. Then she slid into the fitful sleep of maintenance mode, hidden on her rooftop.

She knew she wasn't really dreaming, because she was a robot, and robots don't dream. So no matter how real or bizarre her slumbering images were, in reality, they were memory-read errors in her holographic storage.

Her maintenance programmer-mechanic had been dismissive. "File compression probably caused your consciousness circuitry to overload," he'd said. "I'll clear it up when I have time." But the time never came.

So she accepted it. What choice did she have? Anyway, she wanted to avoid maintenance downtime. The dreams scared her.

She was a robot, and robots did as they were told . . . most of the time. In this area, Geneva had been an expensive experiment. She had been programmed to be independent, to act on her own — and she'd recently decided that her programmer-mechanic's orders didn't matter anymore.

So she had escaped.

Now she was completely on her own, yet her dreams persisted. And they held messages.

As she drifted through sleep — *maintenance mode*, she reminded herself — she was swimming. Foxx was there, purple with rage. The dream morphed into a fight against him. But her weapons failed. She was defenseless when Foxx blasted her.

Then water came rushing in again, filling her up, and . . .

Geneva sat up. The last time she recharged with lightning, she had been knocked out for twelve hours. This time it had been twenty minutes. *I wonder if Charlie's connection to the Hum has anything to do with it?*

CHAPTER 9

Gramercy Foxx sat behind a desk, his back turned to the gathered reporters. He'd been busy. The Future would be released in two weeks.

If only this wasn't so exhausting. It didn't used to be. Foxx remembered a time when he could kill with a word, feast on the ripening soul of a true believer, and still have energy left over to influence the stock market with the Power of Suggestion.

Soon his strength would return. Callis would rule. This time, he would use the limitless reach of technology. He focused on the ancient pool of the Hum, once so deep, and turned to the cameras.

During the "emergency" press conference at the hospital, Foxx had added only the slightest hint of Suggestion to his words. Yet it worked. One week later, millions, perhaps billions, watched on their device screens, hoping for clues about The Future. Even the most jaded reporters were excited, although they hid it.

One woman in the room stood out to Gramercy Foxx: Jane Virtue, a young vlogger. The intense interest on her face caught his attention. It could have been mistaken for professionalism, or a crush, or she might even have been starstruck.

But Foxx suspected the truth had more to do with what he promised: to unite the world in one consciousness.

Foxx could see into Jane Virtue's heart. He recognized the flush of idealism, the hope for a better world.

Jane's skeptical side suspected this was all just a clever marketing slogan, but what if it wasn't? Foxx donated educational software to schools, wiped out hunger in cities across the nation, and gave away free Internet access to the masses. What if he really had found the key to true unity? Her optimistic side wanted to believe.

"Ladies and gentlemen of the world, boys and girls," Foxx began with disarming charm, "The Future is coming, friends, and it will be . . . glorious!" He caressed the minds of everyone who listened.

Jane Virtue forgot the notepad in her lap. She could replay his speech from her mocap recorder anytime. But she would probably hear Foxx in person only once. He had been so reclusive these past few years. He'd never married.

Like the others who listened, Jane felt that Foxx spoke directly to her, comforting her, soothing her fears. So much pain and suffering had ravaged the planet. Maybe it was time for true and lasting change.

After the conference, Foxx's assistants whisked the reporters away. The exertion of Foxx's will tapped his powers, but he would rest and recover. The need for his greatest energy would be coming soon.

CHAPTER 10

Jane Virtue answered her VidFon by simply saying, "Answer call." The earpiece in her stylish-yet-intellectual glasses pumped soothing hold music. The auto-dialer on the other end must have been jammed up with other calls. *Technology.* She rolled her eyes and popped another slice of sushi into her mouth. *Can't live with it, can't . . .*

"Jane Virtue?" the auto-attendant's voice chimed.

"Yes, this is Jane," she said through a mouthful of fish.

"Please hold for Evelyn Rasmussin."

Jane's earpiece piped in music.

"Ms. Virtue, thank you for holding."

"Not a problem." Jane swallowed. "What can I do for you?"

"I am Gramercy Foxx's personal assistant. He'd like to speak with you directly. He follows your vlog. Are you available for a video call?"

Jane was glad she'd swallowed already, or she would have choked. *The* Gramercy Foxx wanted to speak to *her* — not just on the phone but a *video* call!

Get ahold of yourself, Jane. "Yes, I can take the call." Mr. Foxx wouldn't be impressed with her choice of lunch locale — Kwik Sushi, at a discount mall. Mortified, she dashed across the food court. "Can you hold on a minute? I'm kind of . . ."

She almost fell over a baby carriage. "I'm finishing up a story at my desk. Can I, can you, hold on while I go to our . . . conference room?"

She ran through the mall, one hand in her purse digging for her VidCel, the other fussing with her hair. Why didn't she make a habit of primping before she left the office? Because she believed it was more important to *be* professional and compassionate than to merely *look* professional and compassionate.

Evelyn waited patiently as the obviously inexperienced reporter did whatever it was these people did. Evelyn understood that her job was to make sure Mr. Foxx *never* had to wait. If that meant Evelyn did the waiting, it was fine with her.

It was, however, unusual for Mr. Foxx to wait silently on the line, listening to the person dash around, unaware that Foxx could hear every little gasp and clatter. Well, he had his reasons, and it wasn't her place to ask questions.

"Oh, the conference room is taken — there's a board meeting," Jane lied, a little out of breath. "Let me just . . ."

"Not to worry, dear. Mr. Foxx will join the call whenever you're ready."

"Let me check the small conference room. There's no video tie-in, but my VidCel does video OK, if that's all right."

She held her breath. Would her bluff work? And would a changing room at Retro Girl pass for a small conference room? Unlikely, but it was the only quiet, private place she could find.

"Of course, dear," Evelyn soothed. "You're ready for Mr. Foxx, then?"

"Yes, yes, let me just . . ." Jane checked her hair, made sure her nose wasn't shiny, and balanced the phone on a shelf. "I'll activate the video." The lens tracked her face. A clear, steady image projected onto the nearest wall. The fluorescent-green picture horrified her — she looked like a vampire — but then it adjusted again, correcting the white balance to the warm lighting of a desk lamp. Much better. "OK, Evelyn, I'm all set. Do you have video on your end?" She gave her best attempt at a relaxed smile.

Perfect, just perfect. The windows darkened, and Jane appeared on Foxx's wall-size conference screen, just as he remembered her, though her cheeks were flushed from rushing about. The young, idealistic reporter — as long as she spoke the same way she looked, he would have what he needed.

Was that a coat hanger swinging in and out of the background?

He had the call traced to satisfy his curiosity. Information was power, especially if she was to be a central piece in his endgame — a discount mall far from her East LAanges office. Researching a story? Shopping? It made little difference.

How would she conduct herself under pressure? He heard her breathing more slowly. He couldn't let her get *too* comfortable. Another video screen lit up, and his timeless features filled the wall.

Jane fought to keep from gasping. His face looked so unusual on this device! Not at all like the man she'd seen at the press conference. And now she was speaking with him, face-to-face!

"Ms. Virtue," Foxx began silkily, "I hope I didn't interrupt your shopping trip."

Jane blinked. *How did he know?* "Not at all. The seamstress can wait," she improvised. "To what do I owe the honor, sir?"

"Direct and to the point. I like that. I have a proposition for you, dear." *How would she respond to "dear"? Would it ruffle her feathers, or would she warm up?*

She gave him no reaction whatsoever.

"Proposition? You already get more press than football *and* soccer."

"Media ownership has privileges." Foxx leaned in slightly; he was personal, secretive. "I want you to have the exclusive. You can be the member of the press to experience The Future — *firsthand*."

Jane struggled to maintain her poker face. "Well, Mr. Foxx, that's very interesting. But what do you want from me?"

"I want you to see our preparations," he said. "I follow *The Daily Virtue*. It's an impressive vlog. I desire only a truthful opinion from a woman of your integrity."

He was offering her a dream shot. But it was too good to be true.

"Why me? What's your angle?"

Resistance? Excellent. She was sharper than he'd hoped. But he knew she was hooked. "Angle? My dear, there is no angle. May I call you Jane?"

She nodded.

"I don't need more money, power, or influence. I want to give back. The Future will do precisely what I have said. In twelve days, humanity will come together. This is the next step, Jane.

"I've read your articles. I know you're honest. Even to your detriment."

Her *detriment*. So he knew how she'd lost her last big job. They'd fired her after she wrote an article about conflicts of interest on the board of directors.

"What do I have to do?"

"Excellent. You will meet me at my office first thing in the morning, of course. Five a.m. See you then."

His line went dead.

Five a.m.? But that was the least of Jane Virtue's problems.

CHAPTER 11

The Hum was here — it had to be. But people had lost their ability to see it, to feel it. Why would the Hum be so alive for Gramercy Foxx? How did he stay connected? Charlie sighed. *If I understood that, maybe the rest of the pieces of this computer-virus puzzle would fall into place.*

"You said you harness the Hum. What can you do with it?" Geneva asked.

"*Here*, I don't know what I can do. It's like a stream that's run dry — the water should be flowing, but it isn't.

"I'm not accomplished with it yet, although I was learning fast. It's so much harder here! My grandfather can build a shield of energy around a person or animal to protect him. Some people can heal — my mother was very good at that. They say she was a genius."

"Maybe you're a genius, too."

"All my grandfather does is punish me!"

"You need to keep practicing here. So you get strong with it in my time."

"I am. You just don't notice, I've been practicing every minute since I got here. And I *am* getting stronger. Every day has made a difference."

"What else do your people do?"

"Once I saw my grandfather actually disappear. But that requires a lot of emotion. Most of the masters can make things *happen*. The Interrogator says it's unnatural. But the Hum is good. It connects everything in the world. It's the power source! My grandmother said her garden grew from it, and the songs of the universe were more beautiful because of it. Animals could communicate with her, and she attracted them wherever she went, especially wild birds. She could start a fire or put one out, or if she needed wood or water, it would come. I mean, somebody would bring it. Unspoken. But the most important part is *belief*."

"Were people experimenting with it? To see how much they could do?"

"Always. From the beginning of time."

"Which means you don't fully know what it can do, right? Which means we also don't know what Foxx can do with it. . . ."

That sank in for Charlie, right to the pit of his stomach. She was right — they had no idea of Foxx's capabilities.

"Geneva, some people are born better at sports or music. It's the same with the Hum. Some people are born with a much stronger ability to use the Hum. It runs in families."

"You're saying it's genetic?"

"I know it's in my blood. It must be in his, too. Foxx and I have that much in common. I'll give you a practical example of using the Hum. Something simple I can do here in your time. Do you have a coin?"

Geneva put a coin in his hand.

"On my fifth birthday my grandfather taught me this," Charlie said, holding the coin for her to see. "I hope I get this right." He waved the coin in the air, then laid it flat in his palm. "I'm going to make this coin disappear. Watch carefully." And with a flourish, the coin was gone.

"Where did it go?" Geneva played along, humoring him as if he were a toddler. He didn't know her eyes watched faster and more closely than a human's.

"I think . . ." Charlie reached dramatically. ". . . it's right . . ." He snatched the coin from behind her ear. ". . . here!"

"But that's just a trick."

"It *was* a trick." He suddenly became serious. "It's important to know the difference between a trick and the use of the Hum." He pulled the feather from home out of his pocket. "The Hum," he said slowly, "is the true essence of all things." He took a deep breath and began focusing his mind, shutting out all distractions.

Geneva fell silent. She matched Charlie's slow, even breathing.

"My grandfather taught me it is '*the power we all draw upon for strength in difficult times*.'" The coin lay flat in one hand, and he held the feather aloft in the other. Charlie closed his eyes. "Practiced with love in our hearts . . ."

The feather began to tremble. Geneva's eyes widened.

". . . the world opens up . . . and shows us . . ." The coin also began to tremble. The coin rose slowly from Charlie's hand, floating above his outstretched palm. ". . . that *anything* is possible."

The coin floated slowly across to Geneva's outstretched hand. Eyes still closed, Charlie lowered the feather, and the coin dropped into her palm.

The silence and electricity in the air were palpable.

Geneva finally exhaled. "That was real, wasn't it? No trick?"

"No trick."

Amazed, she rolled the coin in her hand and considered Charlie's words.

"That took a lot out of me, though," he panted, putting the feather back in his pocket. "It should have been easy. At home, it would have been simple."

"I've never seen anything like it," Geneva murmured.

"Believe me, it's a small thing. There's something about the energy here that makes it more difficult. My entire life my grandfather said the Hum would disappear. Did it?"

"I don't know. You tell me. And if love is so important to keep in your heart, then how can someone evil — a man like Gramercy Foxx — use the Hum?"

Charlie didn't have an answer.

"So people have used the Hum before to do evil things — but no one could stop them?"

"No one has been able to stop the Interrogator. Some people think he uses the Hum himself. Otherwise, why wouldn't the people he's killing use it to destroy him? Maybe the Interrogator killed my family by using the Hum."

"Who knows?" Geneva said. "Maybe you're more powerful than you think you are. But now it's your turn to learn."

"I *am* learning! For almost two weeks I've done nothing but learn."

"You need to know *everything* about code and computers — *how* they work and *why* they work. Otherwise — Hum or no Hum — we have *no* chance of stopping Foxx."

CHAPTER 12

"Jane Virtue for Gramercy Foxx."

The security guard checked her ID. "Take this elevator to the 200th floor, ma'am."

"Thank you."

The 200th floor reception area was designed to enthrall visitors. A waterfall in the center of the room flowed right to the glass wall, giving the impression of Infinity Falls. It was breathtaking — a waterfall high above downtown LAanges.

"Good morning," said a bright-eyed girl with an eager smile. "I'm Allison, Mr. Foxx's Third Assistant. You must be Ms. Virtue."

"I am," Jane said, feeling very out of place.

"Mr. Foxx will see you right away." Allison led Jane around the corner, past the office of Second Assistant, who did the paperwork, judging from the stacks.

First Assistant Evelyn Rasmussin had an expansive workspace larger than Jane's apartment. Evelyn smiled. "Jane! It's a pleasure to meet you."

"The pleasure is all mine, Evelyn." Jane kept her handshake firm. It was 4:55 a.m. Thank heaven she was on time.

"Mr. Foxx is looking forward to seeing you."

*   *   *

Gramercy Foxx stood. The energy he used for his otherworldly influence hung in the room. Sweet music soothed his guests.

"I hope I didn't keep you waiting long," he said with a disarming smile.

"Not at all, Mr. Foxx." Jane smiled tightly, remaining reserved.

Foxx took the seat next to her at the conference table.

He wants me to feel at ease with him — is it genuine?

"Jane, you're sharp, so no doubt you've analyzed this from every angle."

"My integrity is everything to me," Jane replied. "I will not write or report anything I don't believe is true."

"That's why I picked you! I want you to be *thoroughly* honest! Tell the world what you see and think. You will have more than enough information." He slid a sheet of paper to her. It listed twelve of the most powerful corporate executives in the world — along with their personal contact information.

"These trusted friends are my chief advisers and will cooperate with you in every way. Unfortunately, Terrence Wrightwood has had an unexpected . . . illness."

Jane's eyes widened at the list, although she tried to hide it.

Excellent, Foxx thought. But he wouldn't risk using The Future's full mind control on her. A light touch would be sufficient. He needed the public to believe every word she said.

For the next eleven days, Foxx would keep her preoccupied with the shiny wrappings of The Future, and that would distract her from the truth. He had found the perfect spokeswoman. The world would trust her completely.

CHAPTER 13

"Why did you come get me *now*?" Charlie asked one morning. "You can travel through time, so you could have come for me *any* time in my life. Why did you come now, when I'm twelve? I'll be much more skilled when I'm sixteen."

"That wasn't an option."

"Why not?" Then it dawned on him. "Does something happen to me?"

"Look, I can't interfere with the past."

"But you already *did*! You came and took me away!"

"Yeah, but it's not like that, Charlie. The future is relative, OK? The Interrogator and the people who follow him are . . . dangerous." She let it hang there.

"What, he's going to kill me?"

"I won't say anything more. Foxx is probably going to kill both of us here anyway, so what does it matter? Lighten up. We have enough to worry about.

"So there's one more thing I want to tell you," she went on. "And I can't explain it. For a year, I've been receiving . . . information . . . messages. Usually when I'm . . . in maintenance mode."

"Where do the messages come from? Who sends them?"

"I don't know. I wake up, and I know things."

"Like what?"

"Like *you*. One morning I could see you, or someone like you, where you live, *when* you live. It seemed like . . . instructions. To go fetch you, I think."

"To help you stop Foxx?"

"Well, I don't know. Let me get to that. It doesn't make any sense. I'm a robot. I was built. Programmed."

"You told me that."

"But I didn't tell you *who* programmed me."

"Does it matter?"

"I was programmed by Gramercy Foxx."

"Gramercy Foxx . . . *built* you?"

"I don't know. But he programmed me."

"My *memories* begin in a laboratory in the TerraThinc Building. I remember everything I see, hear, touch, taste, smell — everything. But the information that appears after maintenance mode . . . it doesn't make sense; the messages don't even seem like they belong to me. Memories, dreams, programming. I don't know."

"I wonder what it all means."

"Sometimes I wonder if they were accidentally programmed into me. Maybe Foxx was thinking about something and didn't realize what he put in."

"Well, you've been doing the right thing."

Geneva looked up, surprised. "Thank you, Charlie. You make me *feel* better. And I've never heard of a robot that has *feelings*. I'm different that way, too. Foxx must have gotten my consciousness circuits right, huh?"

"You seem like a real person to me."

"That was the point. He wanted to see how close to a real person he could get and have me still be a robot.

"He gave me special abilities — some he doesn't even understand himself. One of those abilities was time travel. He told me to figure it out with the particle accelerators and magnetic fields and my processing speed. The power levels were right. I just had to practice synchronizing with the energy fields."

"The Hum!" Charlie exclaimed. "You do connect with it!"

"I don't know about that. But eventually I could smash atoms. I could create a portal and *control* it. Getting in and out is the easy part. I had to be able to calculate probabilities. Every one of those lights is another timeline probability vector."

"Geneva, I don't know what you're talking about. Do you know *why* Foxx wanted you to time travel?"

"Sorry. I think he wanted me to take him places. But I escaped. I didn't trust him anymore."

"Why not?"

"He would talk to himself in the lab at night after he put me into maintenance mode. He didn't know I could still hear him. One night he was talking about what he would do when he finally went back in time. 'I'll get even with you, old man,' is what he said. He wants to kill somebody!"

"But how would he know somebody from the past?"

"Sometimes I think he *came* from the past. He's obsessed with it."

"If he came from the past, why can't he go back again?"

"I don't know," Geneva said with a smirk. "At least, I didn't know then. But I think you've made me realize something.

Getting a portal to open the first time is the hard part. After you've done it, then the path is laid, so to speak — there's a weakness in timespace so the portal can reopen, and you can return.

"Charlie, you said the Hum is powerful where you're from, but not here. Maybe he didn't have enough *juice* to get back! I'm nuclear — I've got the juice! Maybe he *made* me to solve his problem. *I can smash through time, and he can't!*"

"You really hate him, don't you?"

"Look what he's doing! He's trying to enslave humanity because he's jealous."

"Jealous?"

"Of his sister. He talked about her during maintenance. She was *way* more skilled than he was. But he's really unhinged."

"You think he wants to go back in time to kill his sister?"

"I don't know. Seems like a lot of effort for a murder. Anyway, he's stuck here, and *I'm* not gonna help him."

"So he's making the best of it," Charlie said bitterly. "He's entertaining himself by seeing if he can hypnotize the entire world."

"Maybe if he does that, his sister will be impressed, and his parents will like him better. Boo hoo."

"Geneva!"

"I have a *lot* of reasons to want to put Gramercy Foxx out of business."

CHAPTER 14

"I broke into Foxx's lab," Geneva said. "I was on a mission. I wanted to see more."

"What did you see?"

"Animals in cages. Experiments."

"What did you do?"

"I ran. As fast as I could. Some robot or animal yelled after me, 'You have to stop him!' I never went back."

"Did Foxx find out?"

"I confronted him. He started dragging me to that room to give me a firmware upgrade! That's the most basic part of any machine's identity, Charlie. He wanted to erase my *identity*! For a robot, it's like murder!"

"Did he do it?"

"No. The closer we came to that door, the harder I fought. Then I managed to pull a portal open right in front of me. *Smash!* Foxx was shocked! I pretty much *fell* into it, headfirst."

"So you got away," Charlie said. "I don't want to make you uncomfortable, but what is the connection between the animal experiments and the computer virus? There has to be a link. Right?"

"Absolutely. And his connection to the Hum is part of this, too. But I don't know how it fits together."

"I think the TerraThinc Building holds the keys to everything. I want to see that lab."

"I don't want to go."

"We are running out of time, Geneva! We have a little more than a week, and a big piece of the puzzle is missing. All of these elements connect somehow into a bigger picture. But until we see it, we can't stop him. We don't understand what we're trying to stop."

"It's very, very dangerous."

"Everything we're doing is dangerous."

"But this is different. When I ran away, he was already designing something new to increase his power. Maybe another robot, like me, but more sophisticated. Deadly. And it's probably in his lab."

"We're in this together. I will be there," he said firmly.

Her response was not robotic at all. She gave him a hug.

"*Friends*," he said.

PART II: FREE WILL

CHAPTER 15

More than seventy thousand people passed through the TerraThinc Building on any given day.

"Nothing's easier than blending in with a crowd," Geneva said. "We'll slip in right under their noses." Charlie found himself jostled along a current of workers rotating shifts through the lobby.

Since the night she'd escaped from Foxx in his lab, Geneva had not been able to use her Smasher portal to get back into the building. Foxx had blocked her. But his traps didn't stop her spying.

She wore a baseball cap with her hair sticking out the back in a ponytail. Today she was an ordinary teenager. "When it clears out, they'll shift focus back to the main entrances. Then we'll go to the lab."

On the 50th floor, they slipped into a dark janitor's closet. "Now we wait."

For Charlie, every minute felt like an eternity. Finally Geneva whispered, "It's time." She handed Charlie a janitor's uniform. "Put this on. It's big, but you can roll up the sleeves."

She hauled an industrial robot out of the closet and pulled

it along behind them. "From the camera's view we're just fixing the bots," she explained. They headed back to the elevators.

She waved her left hand across a black bar, and the elevator light blinked to green. The car accelerated straight up.

"I wirelessly hacked the security network. A spare janitor code will get us to most floors, but the security for the restricted floors will be tricky.

"TerraThinc uses three tiers of security: First, something you *have* — usually an access card; second, something you *know* — like a password; and third, something you *are* — a part of your body that gets analyzed. Biometrics.

"Most of the moderate-restriction areas use fingerprint scanners. Let's hope that hasn't changed."

"What if it has?"

"You don't want to know. So far my chip has worked." She grinned. "Foxx changed the codes on me, but I set up a privileged chip in my hand a long time ago. Precautionary measures. I should be able to pull the new pass codes."

She's nervous, Charlie thought. *So she's talking*.

The elevator chimed. Geneva checked for snoopers, and they stepped into the connecting bank of elevators. She waved her hand and punched 185.

When the elevator doors slid open again, Charlie felt woozy.

"You OK?" Geneva asked.

"This place has bad energy. I can feel it all the way to my toes."

"Let's just get it over with."

"Right."

"Foxx's office is on 200. His living quarters are on 199. His computer lab is on 198, and the animal lab is on 197. The security up there is ridiculous. All three forms of ID — a card *plus* a code *plus* a fingerprint. Nobody but Foxx can get into the animal lab. That's the toughest one."

"When you say you can figure out his codes, what does that mean?"

"I can match his passwords. *And* I have his fingerprints. He didn't think to hide them. Any time I touch a person's hands, I can mimic his fingerprints."

"Do you have *my* fingerprints?"

"Of course."

"How could Foxx forget something as important as that?"

"I'm a robot. I was supposed to follow my programming, remember? There's one big problem. The system keeps track of each card — people can't be in two places at once. So if Foxx's card is on the 10th floor, and then he appears on one of the restricted floors, an alarm sounds."

They loaded back into the elevator, cleaner in tow. She hit the button for the 190th floor and entered the janitor's code. Up they went. No movement from security. The hallways on 190 got mopped every day.

The maintenance elevator doors slid open, and they trudged out. This was the most vulnerable time. If security looked closely, they had a major issue.

They shuffled to the next bank of elevators. Geneva turned away from the camera. She reprogrammed her chip with Foxx's codes. Now, if Foxx hadn't changed his camera kill number, and if security wasn't watching . . .

"I'm counting on your Hum connection today," Geneva whispered.

The main elevator doors slid open, and she waved her hand again. *Green light.*

She punched 197.

Blinking green light.

Seven-digit pass code.

Double blinking green.

Her thumbprint changed to match Foxx's.

Solid green.

They were on their way.

Geneva's greatest fear was Foxx. He kept inhuman hours and rarely slept. Most of the time he worked on the restricted floors. In a nanosecond, any of this could turn sour.

Charlie kept his head down and his mouth shut. The elevator doors slid open on 197, and out they stepped. *So far so good.*

Geneva led Charlie down the hallway to the door. *That* door.

He tried not to stare, but she started shaking.

"Let's go back," he hissed.

"No! You were right — we have to do this. We absolutely do."

CHAPTER 16

Click! The door unlocked. Charlie took Geneva's hand. She squeezed it tight.

They stepped into the dark room. An overwhelming stench of death and caged animals rolled out. Geneva was shivering, but she kept going. She flipped on the light switch.

Animals chirped and squawked, flapping wings against metal bars. Cages lined the walls from floor to ceiling, each dimly lit. Boxes of robot parts were heaped along the walls — arms, legs, springs, tubes, and electric gadgets. Light illuminated the empty operating table in the center of the room.

She knows Foxx programmed her, but she doesn't know if Foxx built her. Of course he did. Look at all these robot parts, these pieces. Yet how could a monster like Foxx create something as good as Geneva? And what did these robots and animals have to do with The Future? How did it all tie together? He felt the room for the Hum but could feel only despair.

"Why is it so filthy?" Charlie asked. "He has all the money in the world. These animals haven't been fed, and half of them don't have water."

"Because he doesn't care if they live or die. They've served their purpose."

"I wonder where his *new* experiment is," Charlie said. "The one to increase his power? I keep looking over my shoulder, expecting it to come after us with an ax."

"I don't know. Stay alert. Let's gather information and get out of here. This place is making me sick."

He was horrified by the macabre menagerie. Dozens of the animals were hybrid — part robot, part living thing.

"Geneva," Charlie called softly, "I think Foxx has embalmed some of these."

"If they rot, he probably can't learn from them," she snapped.

At the end of the row, very small creatures such as insects and worms were attached to computerized parts.

"Look," Charlie said. "These are simple animals — less complicated than a mouse or a dog." Down the row, snakes, lizards, and turtles wore electronic chips. "I wonder if Foxx started his experiments with simpler animals and expanded them . . . all the way to humans?"

"Hey!" Geneva called from the back of the lab. "There's a door here. Let's see where it goes!"

CHAPTER 17

Three floors above the lab, the intercom on Gramercy Foxx's desk buzzed. He let the light blink four times before he answered.

"Sir, McCallum here. They're on the move. They used the old camera kill codes like you said. The robot is monitoring the dummy access codes. I have teams in place. Do you want us to move in?"

"Where are they going?" Foxx asked.

"They're headed toward Restricted Access Two."

"If they're going into Restricted Two, Gargan will handle them."

"Sir, with all due respect," McCallum said carefully, "if they run into Gargan, we won't be able to identify the bodies. I believe it's a young boy we're talking about here. Geneva's the problem, sir."

"Did I ask your opinion?" Foxx's face tightened.

"No, sir."

"Have I ever allowed you to question my authority or judgment?"

"No, sir."

"Then consider this your only warning. You seem to forget that as far as you are concerned, Gargan doesn't exist. But

Gargan has his orders. I suggest you follow yours." Foxx abruptly flicked off the intercom.

Geneva, Geneva, what are you up to, my little runaway? Had the memory wipes failed completely? She had escaped, so obviously the control software had failed. But she must have had partial recall before she disappeared. If that was the case, had more memories returned?

No matter. She would be dealt with. The code had been updated. And she had been a means to an end after all.

He returned to Jane Virtue's status report. She was a wonderful part of the marketing plan. Judging from the ratings on her first three interviews, things were going very well indeed.

Foxx had work to do, but his mind kept returning to Geneva. This should not have even been *possible.* What could she be doing in the lab? It was no surprise that she had made it past security. That was her specialty.

Stop! Do not spin out of control. He focused, returning to the calm center he'd created so long ago he could not even remember its beginnings.

Patience, Callis, patience. It was a fine art. The Future had been a long time coming. And now it was just around the corner.

Geneva, you may yet prove invaluable. He would wait to see what his creation was doing. This boy! *He* was the real mystery, wasn't he?

With a few taps on his computer screen, Foxx updated the program commands for his secret weapon. *Gargan.* They would never see it coming.

CHAPTER 18

The card swipe, code, and thumbprint worked on the next door, too.

Geneva headed for a computer terminal next to an operating table. These animals were a stark contrast to the cacophony in the other room. In better condition, they seemed content. Why were they so complacent?

Charlie read a row of cage labels. "Mouse, rat, bat, rabbit . . . There's an iguana, and a koala. Some of them have names. This cockatiel is Samantha."

The very last cage held a puppy. The label read: Labrador. Unlike the other animals, it did not appear to have any mechanical parts. *Foxx must not have started working on this one.* Charlie put his fingers in the cage, and the puppy licked them.

"Geneva?" He looked back at her.

She was leaning over the glowing computer, absorbed. "Shhhh. Give me a minute. I think I may have found something."

"The Future Code?"

"I wish. These are notes on Foxx's experiments. He was working on animal control. It's right here. He started with hardware implants in brains. Then once it worked properly, he started using less hardware and more software!"

Charlie saw another door. "Geneva! Come look at this."

Something in his voice made her look up. "What is it?"

"Over here. In the very back of the room," he said, his voice catching.

"Yeah, and?"

"This door is labeled 'Geneva.'"

CHAPTER 19

Geneva stood in front of the door.

The card swipe and codes unlocked it. Lights flickered on. Another, larger operating table stood in the middle of the small white room. Metal arms and legs were spread wide and tensed, poised like a Venus flytrap, ready to consume a human-size victim. But there was a different smell here. Geneva placed it. Burned flesh.

It all flooded back.

Strapped down for weeks on end. Feeding time. The smell of gas. Her body, dragged back to that operating table. The prickly fire of metal in her skin. Lying in the small, empty room . . . alone.

Gramercy Foxx loomed above her. An impossibly bright light cast a white fog. But worst of all was the ever-present stench of smoke. Geneva was burning.

"*No,*" she moaned.

"Geneva!"

She didn't answer. *Memory-read errors?* Absolutely not. She was brought here by Foxx to . . . to become . . . what, exactly? The monster had cut her open, wiped away her sense of identity with firmware upgrades, and reprogrammed her. *But why?*

"Charlie, we can go now," she said hoarsely. "We have what we came for." She pulled him into the next room. "He was learning *mind* control, not *animal* control! That's how he was using me. And what we really need to know is not in here." She looked around at the cage-filled room. "I think it's in here."

Geneva pointed at her own head.

She wanted to change the plan.

"Let all the animals go? You're joking!"

She was not. She threw open cage doors, one after another.

Charlie tried to reason with her. "We're going to get caught! Then we can't stop anything!"

"You don't understand what Foxx is doing here! This is monstrous."

"They don't *want* to go," Charlie pleaded. "Look at them. They're not leaving."

"It's mind control." Geneva continued to open the cages. "That's what these experiments are. The animals are *programmed*. Like *me*. I've downloaded the software Foxx used on them. We'll take it with us to study, but I can't leave them here. They've suffered enough."

"We're in the top of a building. Where are they going to go?"

"Just help me. Please!"

Chickens, rats, squirrels, rabbits . . . none would leave their cages. Only the puppy, wagging its tail at the game, followed him.

In a back corner, Geneva found a heavy, locked door. It was labeled "Gargan." She waved her hand and keyed in the code. Thumb. The lock clicked open.

Geneva pushed hard, and the thick steel door inched open. Inside, a familiar low, rumbling sound filled the room. Only a hint of light spilled in. The smell made her nauseated. She reached for a light switch.

That was when she recognized the sound.

Something very large was breathing.

Foxx had electronically ordered Gargan to hold still until the interior door opened. According to protocol, his weapons were inactive to keep the primary target undamaged.

Gargan had crouched opposite the door in tense anticipation for thirteen minutes. He was nine hundred pounds of pure muscle and steel. His long, powerful arms flexed against the ground. He was poised to launch with incredible fury.

Click. The door had finally opened.

Gargan's night vision adapted quickly. A small arm reached in. The thick door opened slowly, revealing a girl.

Zap. The overhead lighting came on, and Gargan's night vision flared to extreme white. *Act immediately. The target must not achieve tactical advantage.*

He launched directly at the girl and shot across the room. His takeoff crushed tile and concrete behind him. His momentum, size, and strength would incapacitate the target.

Geneva was fortunate — the technology in her eyes adjusted to the lighting faster than the black form streaking at her. She switched her hands to gecko mode and pulled. Even with her robotic speed and strength, the door only moved an inch. But it was enough. She fell back.

Gargan hurtled into the thick door.

Kerang! It ripped from the hinges and crumpled. He spun from the uneven impact and fell — directly on Geneva. The last thing she felt was the crush of his unbelievable weight. Then everything went dark.

CHAPTER 20

Gargan's impact was the loudest thing Charlie had ever heard. The walls and floor shook. Glass cabinets shattered.

"Geneva?" Charlie cried.

No answer.

He dashed to the twisted steel door. A huge black gorilla lay in the doorway. Metal implants and heavy steel accessories were embedded in his flesh. Blood oozed from the gorilla's wounded shoulder.

"Geneva?" *This must be Foxx's newest creation.*

A muffled sound came from beneath the gorilla. *She's under there!*

Charlie tugged at the massive body, but it wouldn't budge.

"*Uuuhhh,*" Geneva groaned as she squirmed out from under the weight.

"Are you hurt?"

"Let's open the rest of the cages — fast. Charlie, *hurry up!*"

"McCallum!" Foxx shouted into the intercom as the walls shuddered.

"Sir," McCallum's voice crackled, "I think it was Gargan."

"Of *course* it was Gargan! Keep this quiet!"

"Yes, sir. We're shutting down the elevators. The fire

department is on the way. The building is being evacuated as we speak. Our internal fire response team is coming up the stairwell zip lines to get you."

"It takes fifteen minutes to come up the zip lines!" Foxx barked. "What's happening? Did Gargan get the target, or do I have to go find out myself?"

"The security team on 194 is on the way up the fire stairs to 197. I'll be opening the floor for them. No entry allowed to your lab, sir. We will confirm the targets are neutralized or secure them ourselves in the hallway."

Geneva wanted out *now*.

Boom! Boom! Charlie suddenly felt sick. *The gorilla again.*

Geneva dashed for the elevator.

That was when Charlie noticed the puppy at the far end of the long, narrow hallway. Charlie sprinted to grab it.

"Stop! You'll get us killed!"

He scooped up the puppy and held it close. It wagged its tail. His heart swelled.

"Hurry up, you idiot!" Geneva shouted.

Boom! Boom! Boom!

"*Faster!*" Geneva shrieked from the elevator.

Ka-BOOM! The heavy lab door exploded. Gargan careened out.

Charlie tried to stop, but his feet slid out from under him. He dropped to the ground, skidding with the puppy in his hands. Now he was cut off from Geneva.

The gorilla unfolded to his full eight-foot height.

The Hum! You've been trained your entire life to handle this!

But the gorilla had zeroed in on Geneva. Gargan lunged at her.

Charlie had to help her. *Let go of the fear.* Clutching the puppy, he cleared his mind. As he did, he could feel the change. His skin tingled. *The Hum. It's working.*

Hopeful, he tried a trick he'd been learning at home. He projected the Hum around Geneva to protect her.

Meanwhile, she lowered herself to launch with her cyber-hydronetic legs.

At the right moment, she shot like a crossbow bolt.

Midair, she spun and brought her robotic heel down — a flying sledgehammer.

The gorilla jabbed at her.

The animal's blow glanced off, pushing her aside instead of crushing her.

Amazing. Why is the Hum so strong here? Because of Foxx's lab?

Gargan was still fast, twisting to spin away, but Geneva was faster. She aimed at the shoulder and snapped her heel down. *Sledgehammer, meet open wound.*

Bam! The gorilla let out an unearthly howl.

His right arm shot straight out like a club.

Geneva slammed into the wall, but the Hum field held strong. She bounced inside the bubble as the gorilla collapsed to the ground, a round, crushed section of wall left behind.

Thank you, Grandfather, Charlie thought as Geneva sprang up.

The gorilla clutched his shoulder. A team of six security troops stormed the hallway. They were as surprised to see a giant gorilla as Charlie had been.

Gargan spun to face the new threat and roared.

Charlie was caught in the middle of a showdown. The security team took aim at the gorilla and fired. Charlie hit the floor, holding the puppy close. *They don't see me. They don't see me.* If he made it out alive, it would be a miracle.

Geneva heard the muffled *thwap* of compressed air tranquilizer darts. *No bullets. They don't want to kill it. This must be Foxx's new invention. How crude,* she thought. *How can a big ape help him succeed with The Future? And where's Charlie?*

She was so focused on Gargan that she hadn't seen Charlie hit the floor. She scanned the hallway. Then she punched the elevator button. *Where is he?*

Twelve tranquilizer darts landed in Gargan's hide, delivering a sedative. But he didn't slow down. Enraged, he thundered past Charlie and attacked the team.

"Let's go," Charlie said to the puppy. He scrambled down the hall to Geneva.

"Where did you go?" she asked. "Back into the lab?"

"What do you mean?"

"You disappeared."

"I was flat on the floor. Let's get out of here!"

Behind them, the gorilla was making short work of the guards. Even tranquilized, he was impossible to capture. Six men lay bloody and broken.

Gargan steadied himself and turned to see Charlie and Geneva run to the elevator. The gorilla pushed off the tranquilizer cobweb and lumbered after them.

* * *

Gramercy Foxx watched the hallway video. Why didn't Gargan recognize his men? Programming glitch. He could send a stand-down command. Spare the men.

But that would affect the program-run.

The men would live. Probably.

Geneva hit the lobby button.

The gorilla lurched in their direction, stumbled against a wall, but didn't stop.

The elevator was stuck.

"What's going on?" Charlie asked.

"I don't know, but we're dead meat if I don't figure it out." Geneva closed her eyes, hacking the network. "The elevator's been shut down! I have to override."

The gorilla was twenty feet away.

Charlie frantically punched the button. Geneva wirelessly navigated the labyrinth of access codes and shut-off commands.

"What elevator are we in?"

"How should *I* know?"

Gargan was closing in.

Geneva backtracked to the elevator status monitor. Car 12 was locked out on the 197th floor. Foxx's access code logged her in, and *bang* — car 12 was active.

She hit the lobby button again. The elevator doors slid shut.

The high-speed car began the long descent. They could still hear the metallic rattle as the gorilla pounded on the doors above.

Charlie took a deep breath. None of Foxx's other animals

had made it. He stroked the puppy and could feel its rapid heartbeat. On the back of its neck, two small chips had been inserted just below the skin. *So Foxx did operate on it.*

"Are you OK?" he asked Geneva. "You got flattened."

"I've had better days."

She's lucky, Charlie thought. "And what you saw in the lab?"

"I don't want to think about it. Hey, can you hear that?"

The screech of tearing metal echoed down the cavernous shaft.

"He's coming down the elevator!" she shouted. "We're trapped!"

The ripping noises stopped. Then the elevator car shook violently.

"He's climbing down the cables after us," Geneva whispered.

"Can we get out on another floor?"

"Everything is locked!"

"So it's a race. . . ."

They could only watch the numbers drop: 150 . . . 138 . . . 120.

"We aren't going fast enough!"

The elevator car bounced again, steel groaning. The gorilla descended the cables. Thirty floors passed. Then, after one final lurch, there was silence.

Suddenly Charlie understood. "It's falling! The gorilla is going to fall on us!"

Kaboom! Lights shattered into darkness. The roof crumpled. The steel frame buckled into the concrete shaft walls, grinding the car to an abrupt halt.

Charlie and Geneva collapsed.

CHAPTER 21

"McCallum!" Foxx shouted. "Full report! Right now!"

"Sir, radio transmissions were cut off. The team moved in. We got Gargan, but he didn't stop. Six men down, sir. We're trying to get cameras back online. Blue team is on the way up."

"And the intruders?"

"An elevator went offline near the 15th floor. It was Geneva, sir. With the boy. We don't know anything else."

Foxx hovered over the VidFon, thinking for a moment. "Divert the fire team to the elevator shaft on 197. I want to know what happened."

"Yes, sir. May I speak freely, sir?"

"What is it?"

"What happened up there, sir? Gargan's programming? He did —"

"Exactly what I programmed him to do," Foxx interrupted.

"But my men were hurt up there."

"Then your next set of men better be prepared for *anything*."

"Sir, my men *are* prepared for anything. But they ran into *Gargan*. There is no training for that. I hope none of them are permanently disabled."

"Your men are *hired* to encounter danger. They're paid accordingly."

"But it was *Gargan*, sir."

"Don't let your feelings get in the way of your work, soldier."

When no comment came back, Foxx jabbed the button, ending the call. He closed his eyes and began the slow, deep breathing necessary to access the weakening pool of the Hum. Something was draining it. *It has to be my work in the lab. One more operation, and my new helper will be by my side.* His latest experiment would dramatically increase his connection to the Hum. In fact, his power would be tripled.

He would need it for the big launch.

CHAPTER 22

A dry tongue licked his cheek and brought Charlie to consciousness. The putrid smell of metal and burned plastic made his head hurt. Or had he been injured? He wasn't sure.

The floor was sticky. Was it blood?

"Geneva?" he said weakly.

Her eyes lit up the dark elevator cab.

That *was* blood on the floor. *Uh-oh.*

Drip drip on the floor. The gorilla's arm hung limply through the mangled ceiling, blood collecting at the fingertips. Charlie rubbed the sore spot on the back of his head — just a bump. The blood belonged to the gorilla. Charlie dragged himself to his feet, keeping his distance from the enormous arm.

The elevator doors had pulled open at the buckled floor, leaving a jagged hole big enough for a kid to squeeze through. But then what?

The elevator groaned as it slipped a few inches farther down the shaft.

"You OK?" Geneva asked. Charlie nodded. "Give me your uniform!"

Charlie peeled off the smock, balancing the puppy. Geneva used the thick fabric to cover the nastiest edges of the jagged steel doors. Charlie stuck his head through the opening. They were suspended at least a hundred feet above the bottom of the elevator shaft, wedged between two floors. "Is there any way to get to the elevator doors below us?" he asked.

"First I'll try to open them."

She couldn't tell what floor they were on, so she cracked the security and sent the "open" command to *all* the elevators. Hacked in, she also saw that the elevator crash was bringing security from all over. They were closing in on them rapidly. The doors opened, and she leaped down. "You have to jump now! Leave the puppy behind!" Before Charlie could protest, she added, *"Right now!"*

Charlie peered out the hole. Metal shards all around could slice them to bits. He would *not* leave this puppy. How was he going to climb eight feet down?

He leaned out. *I can do this.* He held the puppy in one arm and stretched the other out to the elevator frame — just beyond his grasp. He wriggled a little farther, brushing it with his fingertips. A little farther and . . .

Screeech! The car heaved. Charlie tumbled out the open doors. He caught himself but almost dropped the puppy. Another shudder and he would lose his grip.

"I told you to leave the dog!" Geneva shouted. "You trying to get us killed?"

"The dog comes, or I don't come!"

"Then grab my hand!" Geneva yelled. "I'll swing you to the ledge! But if you drop the dog, it's your own fault!"

He took her outstretched hand and felt her strength and the strange, sticky sensation of her nano-skin clinging to his flesh.

"Let go when I tell you!"

He swayed back and forth.

"Now!"

Charlie leaped to the ledge. He landed on the edge and tumbled in, the puppy tucked under his arm.

Charlie and Geneva ran to the fire escape and sprinted down eleven floors.

The TerraThinc fire alarm had drawn a crowd. Foxx was big news these days. Reporters buzzed around the evacuating building as Geneva, Charlie, and the puppy quietly slipped through the crowd.

CHAPTER 23

Gramercy Foxx and John McCallum looked down the shaft. Gargan lay on the buckled floor, one leg still tangled in the wreckage of the ceiling.

"Repairing Gargan will be costly," Foxx growled. "Leave me."

McCallum went to see his men off to the hospital. Of the six who encountered Gargan, two were in critical condition. One would never walk again.

John had served his country in the military. Private security simply wasn't the same. Today he had second thoughts about his current employer — he had obeyed an order, and his men had suffered needlessly. That had happened once before. During the war. The consequences had been dire. His conscience would feel better drowned by several shots of Mr. Daniel's finest. Days like today made him miss the stuff he'd sworn off the day he left the service.

Foxx waited for McCallum to go.

Gargan's injuries were severe. Foxx would not spare Hum energy to help him. He didn't like healing anyway. *My sister was always better at the gentler arts*, he thought jealously. *But everything came so easily for her.*

The day's events revealed lapses in security that would be corrected. Gargan's field test fell flat, but McCallum had proven effective. The real question in Foxx's mind was about Geneva. What was she up to? *I made her!* he thought with a flash of rage. *But in programming her genius, did I accidentally transfer some part of myself, my own memories? Details of home? Of my family? My sister?* Geneva knew too much. And the boy. Who was he?

Right now he needed damage control. He would add Jane Virtue to that team immediately. The Future, after all, was only one week away.

CHAPTER 24

"Jane Virtue, *live* with Gramercy Foxx in the wake of the most shocking terrorist attack in LAanges since Chancellor's Day four years ago." She spoke with perfect newswoman diction. Foxx sat behind her on an ambulance gurney, a bandage on his forehead. "Mr. Foxx, the chief of police says the terrorists attacked your private security force. Were *you* attacked?"

"No, no — not compared to my men. Security kept me safe." Foxx offered a tired smile, touching his fake bandage.

"We're grateful for that. What was the motive?"

"It's obvious! We're seven days away from the single greatest social and technological advance of our time. Many people and organizations profit from war and conflict. The Future is a threat to them. It brings unity to all of us."

Foxx lied with practiced ease. Only he and McCallum knew the truth. The security men in the hospital had been given partial memory wipes.

"Perhaps you can share more details about The Future with the public," Jane suggested. "How does it threaten these warmongers and profiteers?"

"Jane, I don't want to reveal more than I have. Terrorists

detonated a bomb today. Fortunately, new buildings like ours are built to withstand attacks."

"Mr. Foxx, thank you for your time. I'm Jane Virtue, live from downtown LAanges. Remember, ladies and gentlemen, The Future . . . is just one week away."

CHAPTER 25

"Hey, stop laughing at my vest. This thing is keeping us safe, Charlie!" Geneva smiled in spite of herself. Any shirt made of aluminum foil *would* look ridiculous. "It stops them from being able to pick up my signal."

"Right. Because of the particle accelerator in your chest. For smashing."

"Smashing *atoms*. Protons race down my arms at close to the speed of light, meet at my fingertips and smash so ferociously that for a split second they create a miniature black hole."

"A quantum singularity of nearly infinite density and energy, where gravity becomes so strong that not even light can escape across the event horizon."

"I can't believe you remember this stuff," Geneva said with a laugh. "But in that instant, I can actually grab the event horizon, and control it. That's how I open a portal."

"Time travel."

"Yeah, or space. Anyway, we were discussing math, remember?"

"Fine." Charlie rolled his eyes. "Nobody can even *do* math where I come from. I'm the best kid around, but it doesn't matter, because nobody *cares*."

"Math made it possible to smash atoms, but math isn't the *point*. Remember, it's just a language. The only language the computer speaks is ones and zeroes . . ."

"Because of the transistors, right?" Charlie interjected. "The computer chips are made of them — little switches that are either open or closed. One and zero."

"Yep. So computers are constantly translating from binary to decimal, hexadecimal to English."

"I understood that the first sixteen times you explained it."

"Hexadecimal. Sixteen. Cute. So you're learning what you need to know. Good. Then check this out." She spun a computer around. "The Code Analyzer processed these slices of the software I got from the archives at Foxx's lab — what he used to program some of those animals."

"That code is different. I haven't seen one like that."

"One column is from a lizard, the other from a mouse. There's a pattern to the information! We can start tracing the similarities between code versions to identify what Foxx has been doing! We can follow the logic trail!"

Charlie understood more and more. Sometimes it astonished her.

On his part, Charlie wondered if technology really was a change for the better. Charlie hadn't once noticed the moon or stars since he'd left home. No wonder the Hum had been forgotten here.

CHAPTER 26

Jane Virtue sipped tea at an informal coffee table as she finished her interview of Janice Wong. They chatted about the most popular subject in the world: The Future. "Your corporation is contributing . . . *what* to The Future, exactly?"

She knew Wong would dodge the question — none of the eleven execs on the list had revealed what The Future was. "I only handle data distribution," Wong said, "but I promise The Future will be impressive."

"Is our global technology capable of handling this?" Jane asked.

"Network connections and power grids are getting upgrades now. The Future will have the smoothest rollout of any web system in history."

"Thank you so much," Jane said, turning to the cameras. "That was Janice Wong on The Future and InterNext. Remember, The Future . . . is just six days away."

All twelve cameras blinked off. Jane was relieved. She thought the HoloStreams made her look fat.

"Jane, I'm a big fan," Wong said. "I can see why Gramercy chose you."

"Thank you," Jane said, genuinely touched. Fame wasn't

coming easily. She had gone from invisible to the home page almost overnight.

Jane had interviewed Janice Wong two years earlier. Wong didn't remember her. But Jane had noticed something different. A spark was missing. CEO pressure?

She checked her VidCel for schedule and document updates.

Good. Gramercy at five o'clock. The Future was looking bright.

CHAPTER 27

Charlie held the sleeping puppy in his arms. She was a girl, and he was utterly charmed.

She didn't *seem* programmed. He felt for more electronic components under her skin, but all he found were the same two small chips on the back of her neck.

"What do you think Foxx was programming her to do?" he wondered aloud.

Geneva stopped poring over the computer codes and nodded thoughtfully.

"Hook her up," she said.

"No wires. Just two little chips."

"Wireless? Then this must be a job for Robot Girl." Geneva grinned. She held a hand over the puppy and closed her eyes. "Ah, yeah. Wrap these wires around her to pick up the signal, and hook her up to the Code Analyzer. Got it?"

Charlie went to work, and Geneva watched, transfixed. The warmth Charlie was feeling was the pulse of the dog's internal radio, which Geneva could read with her own internal radios. How could Charlie sense their ebb and flow?

When the analyzer beeped "all finished," Charlie disconnected the puppy and started playing with her. "What do you think we'll find?"

"The codes from all the lab animals are similar. But each animal's code seems to be a revision of a previous animal, with an added function."

"So what do the codes do?" Charlie asked.

"Different commands. Let's try an electronic command to put her to sleep." Sure enough, the puppy closed her eyes. "I want to see her rev number to get an idea of her capabilities."

"And yours," Charlie added, immediately regretting it.

Geneva fell silent.

She is dead wrong that robots don't have feelings! But as one of Foxx's robots, she would have a rev number, too.

"I'm sorry, Geneva."

"No, Charlie." Her voice was heavy. "You're right. It's just that I *feel* like I'm more than a bunch of circuit boards and wires."

"You *are* more," he said. "How many robots have friends and HoloChats?"

"Probably none. Just like me. Have you noticed any of my buddies dropping by to hang out?"

Charlie felt even worse. "OK, let's move on," he said. *Focus on the task at hand.* "What does the machine do to the puppy?"

"The analyzer runs a full diagnostic on her chips and software. Now I'm ready for mine." Geneva pulled up her ponytail.

Charlie shrank back, but he tried not to show it. Seeing a data jack embedded in her flesh was shocking.

"Are you sure about this?"

She looked over her shoulder and smiled. "Yeah, I'm sure. This is how we follow Foxx's trail. Logic, remember?"

"And when we read your code, and the puppy's code, we'll have a better idea of where Foxx is going with his programming of living things — ending in humans, with The Future, right?"

She nodded. "Six days, Charlie. Speed it up back there."

Charlie connected her to the analyzer. Her hands gripped the chair.

"I'll see you when I wake up." She closed her eyes.

Charlie hooked up the last wire. The analyzer fired away, pumping data into the computer. This time he didn't watch the screen.

Instead, he picked up the puppy and held her in his lap. "You need a name," he said, tickling her tummy. "I'm making up a brand-new word, just for you. Something nice. Calla. No, Callaway. No, Callasee. No, Callaya." She wagged her tail. "You like that one? Callaya?" She licked his hand. "Then that's your name. It's a secret name, Callaya," he whispered. "Just between you and me. OK?"

The puppy — Callaya — jumped happily, almost as if she understood. *Did she?*

CHAPTER 28

"Right away, sir," McCallum's voice echoed from the black box on Foxx's desk.

On a massive screen across the room, Jane Virtue spoke with James Cricket, the CEO of Global Oil. She ran an excellent show. Ratings were record breaking.

"Mr. Cricket, will there be costs associated with The Future?"

"Eventually. You know, one of the remarkable things about Gramercy Foxx is his conviction. He believes so strongly in The Future that the first two months will be completely free of charge."

"But there are those who ask what Foxx is getting in return?"

"Most people agree that free is free," Cricket replied with a laugh.

No one listened to conspiracy theorists. Who would believe there was an effort to control every mind in the world? The louder they shouted, the more Foxx ridiculed them. Control the message, control their minds. The Future is the next logical step.

"Do you mind if we take a call from a viewer?" A VidFon rose between them.

"Of course not." Cricket smiled. Foxx loved this part. Live viewers flooded the lines for a chance to ask inane questions while Foxx charged them by the minute.

"We have Tommy on the line," Jane said, a video image of a little boy on the VidFon. "Tommy is nine, from Great Falls."

"Hello, Tommy," Cricket said warmly.

"Hello, Mr. Cricket." Tommy was nervous.

"Tommy, do you have a question about The Future?" Jane asked.

"My friend said that —" He was interrupted by background voices. "Is The Future a rocket ship to Mars? I think he's wrong."

Cricket let out a Santa Claus guffaw. "I'm not supposed to reveal details about The Future, but I can pretty safely tell you it's not a rocket ship to Mars."

"Thank you for calling, Tommy," Jane added.

The intercom on Foxx's desk blinked. "Yes, Evelyn, send him in."

John McCallum entered, removing his hat. "Sir." He nodded respectfully.

"What do you think of Jane Virtue?" Foxx asked.

"The men in the squad trust her," McCallum said. "That's a good sign."

Foxx nodded thoughtfully. "Your men in the hospital?"

"In recovery, sir." McCallum swallowed. "Postlewhite is out of the ICU. He appears stable. That could change, but the doctors are hopeful. I'm headed to the hospital shortly."

Foxx knew McCallum's true loyalty lay with his men. A good soldier's always did. He needed to change that. He had used a very subtle touch of his Hum influence on Jane Virtue. He would use the same on McCallum.

"I want to find Geneva," Foxx said with the singsong lilt of the Hum. "And the boy."

"We're on it, sir," McCallum said crisply.

"They took something very precious to me when they escaped."

"What sir?"

"One of the animals from the lab. We have a . . . connection of sorts. I have made contact with it."

"How? We've monitored all communications in and out of the building."

"It's not electronic, John. It's more like a psychic connection. I'll need you to stay here. Forget the hospital." Foxx studied McCallum's face for a reaction.

"What are your orders, sir?"

Foxx was pleased. He saw nothing that indicated his Hum suggestion had failed. McCallum would be even more agreeable now.

"Ready the Bird of Stealth. We're going hunting."

CHAPTER 29

Early-morning sun woke Charlie up. "Callaya," he whispered. The puppy immediately looked at him. *Does she already know her name?* "Callaya, come." She did. *This is one smart dog.*

Geneva's voice startled him. "I double-checked and triple-checked, and I still don't understand it. The puppy is a more recent rev than I am. Can you believe that? After all I can do, she just has two little chips. Why bother?"

"Maybe he wanted a pet."

"Yeah right," Geneva snorted. "Newer code should be an improvement."

"Maybe he wanted a really smart pet?"

"Stop kidding around. If the puppy is a more recent rev than me," Geneva said, her voice dropping to a whisper, "then what can *she* do?"

CHAPTER 30

"Take us lower," Gramercy Foxx said in an unnervingly quiet voice.

Most helicopters required heavy headphones and a special microphone just to hear over the noise. But Foxx's stealth helicopter made barely a whisper.

McCallum took the Bird of Stealth 9000 closer to the high-rise buildings.

"A helmet interferes with the mind-spirit connection," Foxx had said. So he sat without a helmet in the copilot's seat, eyes closed, legs crossed like a yogi.

Must help with the mind-spirit connection, McCallum thought with a snicker. The increasing hocus-pocus made everything worse.

"John, you must abandon your disbelief," Foxx said out of the blue. He turned his hands slightly in the air as if he were adjusting an antenna.

Is he reading my mind? McCallum didn't laugh after that.

Passing through five hundred feet of altitude, McCallum flew in tightening circles. *Hunting, Foxx had called it. Hunting a little boy and girl.*

*   *   *

"The puppy's code doesn't make sense, Charlie. It's gobbledygook that goes nowhere. Foxx is brilliant, but I don't get how he could do something so *bizarre*."

"Maybe it's *Hum* code. You wouldn't understand that, right?"

"Hum code? That's not even a programming language."

"So what would you do if this was just *regular* code you didn't understand?"

"I'd start by isolating it, figure out base assumptions. Then I'd feed it varying input to see what comes out. It's called reverse engineering."

"Let's try that." *And we should look at your code more closely, too,* he wanted to add, *although you clearly don't want to, or you would have already.*

"OK. Hook her back up."

*　　*　　*

Gramercy Foxx suddenly screamed in agony, as if his insides had been torn out.

McCallum instinctively yanked the stick back and cranked the throttle. The engine roared, and the bird climbed. *Evasive action.*

Were they under attack? No.

Foxx writhed in extreme pain. He'd torn his seat belt off, and one arm braced his contorted body against the cabin wall. *Is he having a heart attack?*

McCallum reached for Foxx's neck. *Heartbeat? Yes. Breathing? Yes.*

"Mr. Foxx? Can I help?"

Silence.

*　　*　　*

"Wow!" Geneva shouted as the test concluded. Charlie saw it, too. The code colors changed from yellow to red and green. It meant *something*. Callaya had been twitching.

"What is it?"

"I don't know. Something big."

"Are there more tests you can run?"

"A security probe could reveal vulnerabilities . . . *if* this is computer code." She tapped a few keys on the analyzer. "We still don't know. Let's give it a shot."

* * *

"Go!" Foxx gasped, finally able to talk.

"Back to the TerraThinc Building, sir?"

"Yes, yes," Foxx sputtered, struggling to put on his helmet. He hoped it would insulate him from further pain. "Just *go*."

"What happened, sir?"

"Psychic trauma," Foxx gasped. "The dog . . . data over-flow . . . feedback loop!"

Foxx wasn't making any sense. McCallum focused on the bird.

Foxx didn't care what McCallum saw or heard. His mind reeled. The dog's dull glow in his mind's eye had flared as bright as the sun. The blunt force of it might have killed him had the Hum been stronger.

How could two children have turned such a powerful weapon against him? Who was this boy the girl had found? Perhaps he was far more dangerous than Foxx had realized. *If my connection to the dog has been compromised, can this affect The Future?*

Foxx huddled against the passenger door. The glow still throbbed in his head. He wanted to get back to the safety of his office and its electromagnetic shielding.

CHAPTER 31

"Look! Right there." One moment they'd been watching huge green and red spikes of data, and now, suddenly, the screen was blank. "Crazy computers," she grumped.

"What could have changed?" Charlie asked.

"I have no idea. There must be some variable we don't see. Let's rerun the tests."

Curled by Charlie's feet on the floor, Callaya had stopped whimpering the exact moment the images changed on the screen. Her ears had pricked up as if she heard something. At the same time, Charlie felt a light prickling sensation in his toes and fingers. *I knew it. She's been programmed with code — as we expected. But this is different. The Hum. It has to be. But a dog? How does she know?*

Geneva ran her tests again, but Callaya didn't whimper as she had before.

Nothing more happened. The tingling went away. Callaya closed her eyes and went back to sleep. He would have to pay more attention to the puppy.

While Geneva hunched over the computer screen, he quietly tried to do a simple exercise — shift something small in the room. A broken cup caught his eye, and he tried to slide it down a shelf. At first he was unable to connect, and it scared him. *Have I lost the gift?*

He emptied his mind, and when his thinking was clear, he felt the warm flow of the Hum. *Relief at last. Peace and well-being.* The broken cup moved half an inch. Then Callaya woke and watched. As soon as she did, the cup sped up and almost fell off the shelf.

"Can you feel it, too, baby girl?" She wagged her tail. Or was Callaya *helping* him?

"I repeated the tests, and there was no spike in activity. Just one little blip."

"I just used the Hum to move that cup!"

"You think the tests picked that up?"

"Maybe. If they did, what's next?" Charlie asked.

"*I* am," she said simply. "We need to analyze my code. I want your help."

Charlie was surprised how much of it he could read now, and he was stunned by what he saw. But some of the patterns would have been clear to him even back in his own mountain hamlet.

A ballet of abstract bursts of purple, blue, and scarlet opened and closed in a visual song that could only be a manifestation of the Hum. Both Charlie and Callaya moved closer to the screen, feeling the calm warmth of the Hum as comfortably as if they were sitting before a fireplace in winter.

The puppy watched the screen with fascination, as if she were reading and interpreting data, too. Or the Hum.

And maybe that's what she's doing, Charlie thought.

CHAPTER 32

McCallum's security squad carried the exhausted Foxx from the helicopter and up to his 200th floor office.

"John," Foxx rasped. "Spare no expense. In five days, our security must be *impenetrable. . . .*" He struggled to catch his breath. "You must protect us from every possible threat. The Future depends on you."

McCallum watched Foxx try to keep his eyes open. "Yes, sir."

"You must capture them — the girl and the boy. They are traveling with a dog. I need the robot and the dog *alive.*"

"And the boy, sir?"

But Foxx had already drifted into a heavy sleep.

Foxx was trapped in a deep, visionary state. If McCallum had shouted, Foxx would not have heard it. *Memories.* His sister. Always one step ahead. Faster, smarter, taunting her twin brother. He hid behind a tree.

His father's voice. *Your sister excels, but you are incompetent. What's wrong with you? Why are you hiding?*

He knew about the other side. Death. When she passed, he could feel her.

But even dead, she pointed out his inadequacies.

Animals *loved* his sister. And she, in turn, loved everyone. But she did not love *him*. Why should she? He disgusted her. And he hated her for it.

He could hear her chastise him in his head. *Even a dog won't love you! It's little wonder the puppy chose a new master. In the end, you will get what you deserve, Callis.*

But *she* had gotten what she deserved, hadn't she?

I died with love in my heart, you fool. You will die with emptiness.

Die? I will never die! I have cheated death time and again.

But her voice was gone.

It's all in my mind, he thought. He wanted to forget how she tricked him into traveling to a time from which he could not escape. But *those* memories refused to go.

With all her talent, his sister could never have invented The Future. She could never have accomplished such a feat.

His father would have been proud of him.

His success with The Future would finally silence her voice. Very soon.

CHAPTER 33

It was still dark, but Geneva shook Charlie awake. "OK, you were right!"

Charlie opened his eyes. He had fallen asleep on the couch while she examined miles of data.

"My mystery code is connected to the Hum! It has to be!"

"Great! How did you figure *that* out?"

"I analyzed my code and the puppy's. It's the only logical answer. My code is not completely . . . technological, so the Hum code must be woven into mine. And there's even more of it in the puppy — like five times as much! Crazy, right?"

"Amazing!"

"It *has* to connect. We just don't see the lines that connect the dots yet."

"Show me the code, will you?" Charlie asked. "I have an idea."

"I see the Hum," Charlie said quietly, touching the screen. His entire body tingled. "And I recognize some of the patterns from Foxx's office that first night — the streaming numbers and colors and strands of fireworks."

"But the real breakthrough is the nature of the code itself," Geneva said. "Computers are binary. Base-two math, right? This is almost like quantum computers or something, but quantum computers are too unstable to be useful. I've never seen anything like it in use, although I've heard of it. This code uses a base-*four* language."

"Oh, like DNA," Charlie said.

"What?" Geneva's jaw dropped. "DNA? How do you even know about DNA?"

"You told me about it back when you were explaining the difference between a robot and a human. You said DNA is the building block of life. I remember thinking it sounded a lot like what you'd been telling me about computer code. DNA molecules tell each cell what its job is, which means the DNA is the instructions."

Geneva nodded. "Like a blueprint for an entire person, or tree, or whatever."

"DNA tells the cell how to work. And in computers, lines of code tell a program how to work."

"Well, yeah."

"So when you told me that DNA has four possible pieces for each segment . . ."

"Base pair," Geneva said.

"Right. 'A', 'C', 'G,' and 'T,' so that's four possibilities. Hum code. Simple."

"I can't believe the way your mind works sometimes, Charlie," Geneva said. "And I have a computer brain!" She laughed out loud.

"Bear with me, Geneva, OK? I want to look at it the way I look at puzzles."

"Good."

"We *think* Foxx's animal-robot experiments somehow combine computers, living animals, and the Hum . . . to make his final code." Charlie got chills thinking about the possibilities. "And we know he wanted to combine a biological virus with a computer virus. So that has to be connected to DNA. Right?"

"Maybe."

"What you just showed me *is* that combination. But it isn't The Future. It's Hum code inside the puppy. So I'm asking three things. One: What's missing from this code that will be in The Future? Two: How do we stop him from releasing The Future anyway? We know we can't hack into it. You've already tried that. Right?"

"Unfortunately."

"Question Three: How do we use this code to stop Foxx? How does it help?"

Charlie picked up the dog. "We've come so far. I feel like the answer is right in front of me, but I can't see it!"

He allowed his mind to step back and process the whole landscape. Like pieces in a jigsaw puzzle, the elements began to make a picture in his mind.

"One of the more difficult things my grandfather taught me was to use the Hum to open my intuition about languages. I've only tried it once, but it allowed me to understand what he was saying in another language."

"So you can translate?" Geneva asked.

"Something like that. Grandfather spoke French, which I don't speak, but I could understand him. Not what he said to *someone else* — only what he said to *me*."

"So, if you speak English," Geneva asked, "and somebody else speaks another language, you understand each other? But *just* each other?"

"Right. When Grandfather taught me, I didn't do so well. But it's worth a try."

"What do you want to translate?"

"*You.*"

"Huh? What do you want to translate about me?"

"If computer code is a language *you* understand, and the Hum is a language *I* understand . . ."

Geneva nodded.

"And if this Future code is made up of both computer code and Hum code, I might be able to understand it — because you can understand computer code, and I can probably understand the Hum code. Does that make sense?"

"If it makes sense to you, it's worth a shot."

"We still don't have a way to stop Foxx even if we can translate The Future code. But if we understand the puppy's code, maybe we can understand The Future code and think of a way to stop it."

"What do you need?"

"I'll need your code, since it'll be like translating something you're saying."

She activated the Code Analyzer. He recognized the part that was Geneva's computer code, and he *felt* the part that was the Hum code.

Nothing happened. The computer language in front of him was too strange to understand. "I'm sorry, Geneva. It won't work. French was a lot easier."

"Don't give up. It's a great idea. You can *feel* the Hum, right?"

Charlie looked over at Callaya. "Wait! The puppy!" He picked her up.

Geneva sent the code across the screen again, and Charlie immediately felt the difference. The Hum didn't just tingle. It *flowed.* It rushed from his toes to his fingertips. *This was it!*

Charlie locked his mental energy on the lines of code. Within seconds, the nonsense shifted from a jumble to something more. The code was *changing*, translating into a language made up of computer code, DNA, and the Hum.

PART III:
GENEVA'S SURPRISE

CHAPTER 34

On the roof of the Texifornia Bank Building, Charlie shuddered. He'd had enough of heights after Foxx's windows at the top of TerraThinc. The wind gusted.

Only a few buildings stood as tall as the Texifornia in the LAanges skyline, and TerraThinc towered over them all. Charlie had a great view. He used the camera on the VidCel to zoom in on Foxx's brightly lit office.

Charlie was utterly alone. Geneva had left two and a half hours ago. He hadn't wanted her to go back into TerraThinc, but she was right. The Future code would be complete. They had to break in to access it.

Geneva had given him a VidCel, a tablet, and instructions for texting, video chat, and email. He rehearsed the touch-screen moves. He just hoped the video chat worked. Geneva wasn't sure how well it would function up here.

"Charlie!" Geneva's hushed voice came out of his headset. "I'm in!"

"Great!" *She can't hear me.* He hit the CHAT button. "What happened?"

"Some falling garbage and junk hit me, but I made it to the 198th floor."

Since their previous break-in, Foxx had drastically increased security, but Geneva had found one vulnerable spot: the recycling system. Infrared and motion detectors had been installed, but they hadn't been connected to the main security system yet. This was their last chance.

From the basement, she had climbed up the series of chutes to 198. Magnets tugged on her, but they were mainly an irritation.

"I don't tire easily, but I *stink*. People really shouldn't put garbage in with the recycling. I'll hit you back when I'm ready."

How can she be in such good spirits?

"OK, I'm on the move."

Charlie hit the CHAT button. "Good luck."

"I'm sending you the video feeds from the cameras. Keep an eye out."

Eight video feeds and alarm indicators came up. Now he could see different angles of the TerraThinc Building from the inside. "Got them."

"Watch 23. *Closely.*"

An empty hallway. Then a closed door slowly cracked open — just an inch.

"Can you see me?" she whispered.

"Yes, a little."

"Do you think anybody will notice?" She had twenty yards of hallway to get to Foxx's computer lab door. That was a long way to go, even camouflaged.

"I don't know," Charlie whispered. "But they watch a lot of cameras, right?"

"Yeah," she said, unconvinced. "Here goes."

The door opened two more inches. Charlie could just make out a glimmer of light reflecting from her eyes.

"Motion detector!" She froze. "They got me!"

Charlie saw it. The motion detector had triggered an alert.

"Is anyone coming?" Geneva only had a few seconds to get down the hall. It was too risky. She pulled the door closed again.

"I don't see you now. What are you doing?"

"I have an idea. It's either really brilliant or really stupid. Diversion time." Then the video feeds went dead.

"Geneva!"

No answer. Her voice was gone.

*　　*　　*

Chaos!

John McCallum nearly threw his coffee across the room. After three all-nighters, he wondered if he was hallucinating: One second, all systems were normal. The next, every alert lit up, every siren blared. Either they were under a massive full-scale attack, or all of the upgrades crashed. He hoped it was an attack.

Three supervisors were yelling at once.

"What happened?" McCallum shouted. "One at a time!"

"Every camera has gone down!"

"Two Unix experts say this is a directed, multifaceted attack."

"Sir! All systems have gone offline."

McCallum could smell the fear on his team. He needed a supervisor from Elite Group — Foxx's private physical security — not these night-patrol clowns.

He had a thought.

"Bring it down," he said quietly. "Bring it *all* down."

Was it a serious attack? Or had the whole system crashed? Either way McCallum's best bet was to shut the whole thing down and reboot. They'd lose a couple of minutes of security, but they would be functional again.

That's what Geneva was hoping for. It had worked! By using raw electrical noise masquerading as real computer data, she had shut down the entire network.

Now she'd have two or three seconds of total power outage to get into the computer room — Foxx's inner sanctum. She'd have full access to everything.

Three days until The Future. The code must *be ready.* Foxx wouldn't cut it closer. And now she'd be able to read the data. *I just have to get out alive.*

McCallum knew it was coming. Foxx's direct line rang.

"Yes, sir. Systems are coming back online now. We're checking the logs, and . . . No, sir. I haven't authorized *any* action since we don't know . . ." He took a deep breath and closed his eyes. "I'll give the order." He changed phone lines. "Full alert status," McCallum barked. "Deploy security spiders throughout the building. Get an Elite team ready *now*. I want up-to-the-minute details on the spider-bot data."

McCallum scanned video monitors for terrorists, corporate mercenaries, even a robot squad. *Nothing.* Whatever was going on, he hoped Geneva and the boy weren't behind it. Foxx's orders were clear, but "take them alive" wasn't comforting.

CHAPTER 35

Geneva sprinted into the computer room. *Suh-weeet! It worked!*

Emergency lighting came on. But the electromagnetic locks didn't open. Luckily her access codes worked before the new systems kicked in. *Click.* She slipped into the beating heart of the monster's deepest lair.

Charlie hit the CHAT button repeatedly. No response.

The entire building had gone dark. Video down, chat down, lights out . . . What had Geneva done?

Slowly lights flickered on throughout the building.

"OK," Geneva's voice finally crackled. "I'm in."

"With the computers?"

"Right. But very vulnerable."

"What happened?"

"Can't talk. Let me know if any cars show up outside — we don't want visitors. Have the video camera ready. Remember, no news is good news."

Charlie was on his own.

Blink. The security screens came up, and he watched for trouble. Nothing.

Meanwhile, thousands of security spiders deployed. Less than a half inch across, on Charlie's screens, they were invisible. He had no idea they were there.

Geneva had seen some powerful computers. She herself was an amazing system. But looking at Foxx's supercomputer was awe inspiring. She used one of her arms as an inductor to read the magnetic field surrounding the tall black cabinets. The amount of electricity used was off the charts.

She had to get into it. Username and password. What could they be? The cursor blinked at her. *Enter the right code, and you're in, little robot girl*, it taunted. *Enter the wrong code, and a squad of giant gorillas will eat you.*

She still had Foxx's security card, username, and password. His password would almost certainly have been changed. But there was always a chance.

She swiped the card. The cursor blinked ominously.

USERNAME: _

GramFoxx, she carefully typed in.

PASSWORD: _

The machine blinked again.

She took a deep breath and entered Foxx's password. Once it was Foxx Supreme, but now he spelled it F0xx_$upr3m3. Geneva hit ENTER.

INCORRECT USERNAME/PASSWORD. TRY AGAIN.

She wouldn't get many tries before the system locked her out. Usually five.

Security types tended to change passwords instead of usernames, so she thought long and hard about her next move.

Gr@m3rcy_$upr3m3.

INCORRECT USERNAME/PASSWORD. ONE ATTEMPT LEFT BEFORE LOCKOUT.

She cursed under her breath. Only three tries — security was that tight.

If she could rule out a few letters, she'd have a better chance at guessing the password. She tested the springiness of each key with her sensitive fingers. The less springy, the more times that key had been pressed.

She also examined the letters on each key. The more worn, the more times the letter had been used. Foxx tended to do most of his programming using voice commands, so the keyboard was used most often for passwords.

She calculated the results. The only letter that didn't fit the old password was *L*. Foxx had changed something — a word or code that used the *L* key multiple times.

What could it be? *People usually choose passwords based on things they can easily remember — a pet's name, or a birthday, or a street.*

It would probably be a short word, or other letters would have shown more wear. Holly, hall, well, sell, loll, lol, cell, call . . .

Call. Why did that sound familiar?

The night Foxx had taken over the virus writer's mind, the guy said his master's name was . . . Callis. Right! It was worth a try.

USERNAME: _

She typed GramFoxx. Slowly. No mistakes. This was her last chance.

PASSWORD: _

She held her breath. Then she carefully typed in:

C@ll!$_$upr3m3.

The cursor continued blinking. Her heart raced. Any second a squad of security goons could burst in and grab her.

The screen flared to life, and line upon line of code ripped down the screen.

"Welcome, Mr. Foxx," said a silky voice. "Shall we continue?"

Geneva couldn't believe her eyes. She did her best Gramercy Foxx impression: "Yes." *The Future. This was it.*

More code spilled by. She jacked into a dataport and hit ESCAPE. The flow stopped, and Geneva began typing. She started with "Help." *I need to know what kind of system this is,* she thought. Pages of help scrolled across. She was ready. Then she began typing commands as fast as the computer could handle them.

Charlie paced. *No news is good news.* That didn't help. On the video screens, armed security guards were quickly assembling in the basement. *This could be bad.*

Movement on the ground caught his eye. Vehicles were screeching into the TerraThinc parking structure.

"Geneva, we have a problem!"

CHAPTER 36

McCallum watched the data feed. Information from ten thousand bots had come in from all five types — motion, audio, EMF, heat, and the fifth, which Foxx himself had designed. The spider-bots had covered the entire building, except for the most secure areas. Even micro-robots couldn't squeeze through security doors. But they gathered enough information through the walls to paint a picture.

The building was secure. The high-security areas showed nothing unusual. In Foxx's computer room, electronic activity and infrared hot spots were normal.

There had been no attack. A catastrophic security system error had crippled the building. Someone knocked on his door. It was Physical Security and one of the guard-techs. The worker sneezed. McCallum instinctively backed away.

"Sir, Steinikov has something to report — an anomaly just before the outage."

"And?"

"Well, sir," Steinikov began nervously, "a motion sensor triggered on a security floor. I flagged it for follow-up, and . . ."

"What floor?" McCallum snapped.

"Floor 198, sir." He sneezed again. "I stepped away to take my medicine. Then the whole system went crazy. Those sensors trigger all night long — false alarms from temperature and pressure changes. I forgot until I updated my logs."

McCallum was already reviewing the logs. Sure enough, on 198 a motion sensor had triggered just before the crash. He pulled up video for the hallways and sent bots to probe for more information.

Then he noticed the one detail everyone else missed. Halfway down the hall, a white-on-white door moved. A sliver of black appeared. The door cracked open from the inside — only an inch, but enough to trigger an alarm. McCallum had a horrible sinking feeling. It was the recycling system door. He zoomed closer. Within the shadow, a point of light glimmered.

He enhanced. A lighter color filled the inch of darkness. Someone *was* in there. Someone short. *Geneva*. Whatever she was doing had wreaked havoc on one of the most advanced security systems in the world.

"Assemble my team. And get me a perimeter. I want spiders in the recycling chute. Right now. The entire building is on total lockdown."

Spider-bots swarmed the chute. It was empty. A small person could scale it to reach the upper floors. He kicked himself for making that system a lower priority.

The bots scanned through the walls, ceiling, and floor of 198. Foxx's computer room had a visitor.

McCallum braced himself to make the call.

"We've got her. On 198. I think it's only the robot. The boy does not appear to be on site. Yes, sir. We'll see you there."

Geneva. McCallum snapped his helmet shut and grimly put on his gloves. Sometimes he hated his job.

CHAPTER 37

Geneva didn't have time to be amazed. Foxx's private codes poured out of the system. She had them *all*. The Future was hers.

She decided to add a little surprise of her own to the mix, too. Her fingers flew. She was on Foxx's system. Her addition would be indistinguishable from anything Foxx or Yates had written.

There was only one problem. Foxx's security force was mobilizing. She should get out *now*. But she wasn't finished. *I may escape yet, if Charlie can pull off his end of the deal.* She brought him up on chat.

"Get out! *Get out!*" Charlie screamed. *"They'll destroy you! Your firmware!"*

Geneva was cool and calm. "You're doing great. Listen, I need you to . . ."

It got worse. Charlie's video feeds went dark: Remote Host Unavailable.

Buzz. It was the VidCel. His palms were sweating.

"What you need to do . . . I've got the . . . hurry and . . . download code . . ." Geneva spoke so fast he couldn't catch everything.

"Geneva! Forget the code! Get *out!* Right now! They're *coming!*"

"Let them come. This is gonna work. InterNext is down, but I'm sending data over the cell. Is it receiving?"

Transfer complete. "Yeah, it's done."

"Four codes sent. But the next one is *huge.* They're going to jam the signal."

File transfer. The blue line crawled across the tiny cell screen.

"No matter what, follow the directions. I'm counting on you," Geneva said.

Security was moving in.

"Wait! I can't do this by myself! I need you!"

"Just remember —"

Click. She was gone.

File transfer failed.

CHAPTER 38

"Cell jam complete, sir. We traced a call in the building."

"Explain," McCallum replied.

"The point of origin is an upper floor," the IT guy said. "We estimate the call recipient to be a block or two east, six hundred to a thousand feet up."

McCallum was impressed. To the east, there were only four or five tall buildings, unless the subject was in a helicopter. *Unlikely.*

Tech security had blocked all unauthorized data flowing in and out of the building. "Several streams are still attempting to get through. They're probably legitimate, but we're cross-referencing all hardware addresses."

"You have two minutes."

McCallum and Red Team rode up the only two active elevators. The building was on lockdown. No one in; no one out. Not even data.

Ding. The elevator door opened. Floor 198.

"Weapons nonlethal. Do not fire unless I give the order."

John McCallum entered the hallway with his security team one step behind. He took in a sharp breath. The hall seethed in a crawling, surging mass of robotic bugs, writhing on the walls, ceiling, and floor. It reminded him of a horror movie.

Even more disarming, the spiders cut a wide berth around a single figure: Gramercy Foxx.

CHAPTER 39

Security was closing in.

With Charlie safe, there was still hope. And Geneva's contribution to The Future would be untraceable. She didn't have time to test it, but time would tell.

What? Charlie couldn't believe what he was reading. *Hum code.* And Geneva wanted him to deactivate it?

But there was no time! This was crazy! He didn't have the Code Analyzer or Callaya to help him!

Panicking won't help. He slowed down and cleared his mind. Then he opened the files she sent.

Geneva was counting on him.

CHAPTER 40

Geneva could actually *feel* the broadcast field turn off. Magnetic, electric, or Hum, it shut down. A tingle in her circuitry was suddenly gone.

Charlie did it!

It was time to make herself scarce. They'd locked her out of everything except the air-conditioning and lighting controls. She'd anticipated that.

She was about to log out when she noticed an innocuous-looking file on the storage area network — a file called Virtue. Geneva knew she should bolt. Still, knowing more about Foxx's spokesperson might be one more tool to stop him. She decided to take the risk and grab that file before she slipped out of the room.

Geneva wasn't the only one who had felt a change when Charlie shut down the Hum field that prevented Geneva from smashing atoms.

Foxx felt it, too. But he was unconcerned. *It has to be the boy, and he thinks he's accomplished something that matters.* Foxx even smiled. There would be no time travel, no escape for his runaway today.

*   *   *

"Blue Bird is airborne." The helicopter pilot called in to McCallum, who was busy on Floor 198. If the mystery caller was on a roof, McCallum would know soon.

Outside the lab, Gramercy Foxx demanded a moment of silence. None of the men were allowed to look at him. Foxx began to speak in a quiet, singsong voice. Foxx's body moved in rhythm with the sound.

What is he doing? McCallum suddenly felt woozy, as if he'd just gotten off a roller coaster.

He felt he could almost *see* Foxx's voice. The air in the hallway thickened until it made him claustrophobic. The sudden nausea reminded him of his whiskey nightmares. He fought it.

How was this affecting his men? His readouts blanked, as if they'd overloaded. There was no explanation. He thought of the strange, unexplainable helicopter incident. And then it was over.

Foxx was looking straight at him, strangely calm. Waiting.

McCallum gave the order. The door swung open, and he led his team into the computer room.

CHAPTER 41

On the roof, Charlie was having a mini-celebration. He had never felt so attuned to the Hum. The code Geneva sent him had become so clear that he instinctively knew how to block it. It was as simple as snapping his fingers.

But then he sensed a surge in the Hum. It started as a rumble. He didn't hear it, he *felt* it — a massive force he didn't think possible in this time and place.

The entire TerraThinc Building emanated a Hum glow so intense it blotted out the building altogether. *What was going on?*

Geneva had just climbed into the air duct before the door burst open. Five armed men jumped into the dark computer room. Even with night-vision goggles, it would take several seconds to spot her. She was in full camouflage, above their heads and clear across the room.

McCallum scanned the rows of computer racks. Long runs of cable rails snaked their way through the mazelike room.

"Clear, clear, clear, clear!" His men confirmed the room was empty. Spiders flooded in.

The thin metal of the air duct had popped noisily when Geneva crawled in. She didn't dare move again. They'd hear her for sure. Barely breathing, she listened to the soldiers. But another sound distracted her — like dry leaves in the wind. Or thousands of tiny robotic bugs. She needed a plan. Fast.

The sensor bots easily found her. McCallum pointed his Mark V at the duct where Geneva was hiding. "We know you're up there, Geneva. Come on down, nice and easy."

She recognized McCallum's voice but didn't intend to climb down nicely *or* easily. Her digital map of the air ducts showed a straight run for fifty feet into the ceiling above the next room. If she could make it there, she might have a chance.

Hands and feet in gecko mode for extra traction, Geneva dashed forward.

CHAPTER 42

They heard the pop-popping of sheet metal. She was making a run for it.

"Energy weapons on stun! Light her up!" Five beams of Mark V plasmonic electricity hit the duct.

A blast from the Mark V fried electronics. Cars died. It was *highly* effective.

Except against a robotic girl who considered it fun to get struck by lightning. She soaked up the power, topping off her stores.

"Cease fire!" McCallum yelled. The girl hadn't missed a beat. When the electrical storm stopped, he even heard laughter. "What on earth?"

His men stared, dumbfounded.

"You three with me. Ramirez, get into that duct!" Jorge Ramirez was smallest. McCallum and the other three ran into the hallway.

Geneva dropped into the next room — another computer lab. Limited exits. There was only one viable escape route. The Smasher portal should be *above* her.

The door burst open. "On the ground! *Freeze!*"

The four men seemed to move in slow motion, but this time their weapons would fire bullets. They would tear her insides apart. She needed three seconds.

"*On the ground!*"

Geneva's mind-splitting siren ripped the air. "*RRRRRRRrrrrrooooooooowwrrrrrrrrr!*"

It nearly burst their eardrums and sent them to their knees in agony.

Someone fired. Bullets ricocheted. Geneva dodged around a row of computer racks. She skidded to a stop and touched her index fingers together.

"See you later, McCallum!"

But nothing happened.

She tried again. "Come on, *SMASH!*"

Again, nothing. *But I'm fully charged.* Charlie had disarmed Foxx's blocking field . . . she'd felt it! *What am I missing?*

It was too late. *Click.* A gun cocked behind her. "Turn around, slowly."

She did, hands in the air. McCallum found himself marveling at Foxx's handiwork, yet the man's motives were deeply disturbing. Why build a robotic girl? She looked so . . . normal.

Geneva sized him up. "You don't know what he's doing, do you?" Her voice cut through the ringing in his ears.

For the first time in twenty years, McCallum found himself off-balance, uncertain.

"I'll take it from here." Gramercy Foxx appeared from nowhere. He placed one cold hand on McCallum's shoulder.

Geneva's eyes filled with terror. McCallum felt her pleading. But he looked away. His men were rubbing their ears.

Ramirez dropped out of the duct. The walls and floor swarmed with bots. Lawrence Yates stood by a computer terminal, staring vacantly. How had they missed seeing him? McCallum called out orders to his team, but in his heart, he felt a sinking sense of disgust. *Have I become a coward?*

Geneva's teeth began to chatter. She had no plan, no escape, and no hope.

"Geneva, my dear, dear girl. I've missed you," Foxx said. "Confused? Ahh, no time travel to escape. I *gave* you the ability to smash atoms. I also *took it away*. I created you. Like me, you are now *stuck*. The doors to the past and future will not open to you again. There is a power greater than your brilliant technology: *me*."

So Foxx had disrupted the fields *himself*.

"And the boy?" Foxx asked smoothly. "He is nearby? Security intercepted your call. They're fetching him. We'll *all* be together soon. John, you may leave now."

McCallum hesitated. *I'm leaving a child with a monster.* Then he reminded himself: *She's not a child. She's a robot.* He snapped his fingers and led Red Team out.

"My dear," Foxx cooed, "you've almost *changed* since I built you. How can that be? Soon, we *will* get to the bottom of your . . . rebellion. And I will correct it once and for all." The terrifying authority in his voice chilled Geneva to the core. "Enjoy these moments of free thought. They'll be your last."

Geneva scanned the room for an exit.

"Don't even consider it," Foxx purred. "Welcome home. I am so relieved to finally be reunited with my *daughter*."

* * *

As Foxx spoke, Geneva opened her final line of communication with the outside world — the building's lighting system. She tapped in wirelessly and hoped Charlie was ready.

On alternating floors, she turned the lights on and off, sending her last message out. Morse code.

Would he get it? Had he been caught?

CHAPTER 43

Charlie heard the helicopter before he saw it. He dropped the tablet into his bag. Crouching low, he held the VidCel up to record.

Geneva had told him this would happen. Every window facing Charlie lit up and flashed. He recorded all of it. The lights blinked in a pattern Charlie didn't understand. But the phone did. It had been programmed to decrypt Geneva's message.

CAPTURED. STAY HIDDEN. THEY'RE COMING FOR YOU. TURN OFF PHONE. GO TO HIDEOUT. FOLLOW INSTRUCTIONS WHEN SAFE. GO NOW.

Then the building lights went dark.

Captured? No, no, no! *It wasn't fair!*

The helicopter's spotlight searched the rooftops, circling closer. He had to run, or they would catch him, too. Everything depended on it. If he didn't get away, Foxx would succeed. All they had done would be wasted. He dashed for the stairwell.

The spotlight caught him. He wasn't fast enough. The chopper dropped low.

Charlie shielded his eyes from the bright light. The pounding of the rotors shook the rooftop.

A rope line dropped down. Armed men leaped out.

✳   ✳   ✳

"Sir, we've spotted the boy. Blue Team is giving chase."

McCallum's heart sank. He had hoped the kid would escape.

"Blue Team Alpha! Intercept in stairwells," McCallum ordered. "You four, come with me. You three, stay here. Ramirez, you're in charge."

"Permission to speak, sir?" Ramirez asked. "This is a *boy*, sir. May I ask why we're pursuing him?"

"That *boy* invaded Foxx's building and blew it up the other day."

"The *terrorist*?"

"Yes, the terrorist. Now, get going, Ramirez." The elevator doors closed.

Was there any way the poor kid could escape?

Charlie's legs shook terribly.

At the top of the stairwell, a Mark V plasmonic blast had glanced off his right arm as he bolted through the door.

Thirty desperate floors later, he paused to explore the wound. It hurt — no, tingled — but it wasn't serious. The blasts continued during his descent, but Charlie wasn't hit.

His fleet-footedness saved him. The soldiers' heavy weapons and backpacks slowed them down. Charlie paused to catch his breath, leaning out to look up and down the center of the stairwell. The airway stretched from the ground to the roof more than ninety stories up. The soldiers weren't far behind. He thought he could outrun them, but another sound caught his ear.

Many floors below, hands grabbed the rails, climbing up the stairwell toward him. Another team of soldiers would cut him off!

Charlie grabbed the handle of the exit door. It wouldn't open. He was trapped.

Charlie ran on. He yanked on the exit door on each floor, but they were all locked. He hurtled down the stairs with reckless speed. There was nowhere to hide — no trash cans, no piles of rubble — nothing but stairwell, railing, and wall.

He skidded to a stop.

The men above were still racing toward him. In a minute or so they'd reach him. Below, the soldiers were even closer.

Floor 36. He was still really high up.

In his pocket was the feather from his demonstration to Geneva. The Hum hadn't been working well for him in this time and place. If not for Callaya, Foxx would have crushed him. *Callaya, I wish you were here!* But she wasn't. He saw no other choice.

Grandfather, help me.

Charlie climbed onto the railing.

The stomping boots above slowed. The men stared down at him.

"Kid, don't jump! We aren't gonna hurt you!"

Right, Charlie thought. *That explains why your guns are all pointed at me*. He clutched the feather to his chest and closed his eyes. He slowed his breath until he reached an inner calm. He tuned out the shouting and the boots.

Quietly he began the words and rhythms to pull the power of the Hum into him, through him. His spine tingled.

Believe . . .

The men were getting close. He had to hurry.

But that was against the very nature of the Hum. *No rushing.*

Allow the Hum to happen, Grandfather said. Now Charlie's life depended on it. Lots of lives depended on it. *Geneva . . .*

But he couldn't think about that. He couldn't think at all. He had to simply breathe into the energy — into the Hum. Let the words and music flow. He had to simply *be*.

I have to believe.

Believe . . .
Believe . . .
Believe . . .

Garcia got there first.

The boy was just below, balanced on the railing. His eyes were closed. *The kid's gonna jump. He's gonna jump, and my job's on the line. Capture him alive. Gotta capture him alive.*

The boy leaned out into space.

Garcia flung himself off the stairs. He intended to tackle the boy. But he was too late.

The kid stepped into the void and dropped like a rock.

Garcia felt the tips of his fingers brush the kid as he hurtled by. He reached after the falling body, heedless of his own safety.

His partner, Molina, was a few steps behind. He lunged in a futile attempt to grab the kid also. He shouted to the men below.

Arms stretched out, trying to catch him. Snag a piece of clothing. *Anything.* But gravity pulled harder and faster. Charlie plummeted toward the ground.

Six helmeted heads leaned out over the railing, watching a little boy fall to his death. Not one of the professional soldiers could believe what happened. Nor could they fathom how he had stepped off the railing with such calm. No flailing. No scream of terror.

Just a boy with one arm held to his chest and the other raised above his head, palm flat and motionless, except for the terrible speed with which he descended.

Believe . . .
Believe . . .
Believe . . .

CHAPTER 44

"What do you mean, he *jumped*?"

"The kid jumped, sir," Molina said, still winded. "Call an ambulance. Or the morgue. No one could survive that fall."

McCallum closed his eyes. *That poor, poor kid. What have I done?*

But when he arrived at the stairwell, there was no kid. No dead body. Not so much as a blood smear.

"I don't understand, sir! The kid stepped into open air from thirty floors up," Garcia said, dumbfounded.

McCallum had no choice but to believe his men. The events of the last few weeks were blurring his sense of reality. *What is going on?* "Find the boy!" he commanded. "Fan out. He can't have made it far." Silently, however, John McCallum was pulling for the kid. *Go, kid, go.*

Charlie's arm still tingled. *Where am I?*

The stairwell was gone. He was outside. Wind whistled lightly through the trees in the cool night air. The breeze took him back to his mountain, where the Hum flowed freely and strongly.

What happened? The whole world had gone insane.

Then it came back to him.

Charlie smiled. *It worked.*

Allow the Hum to happen, Grandfather had said. His belief had taken him from the stairwell to a safer place. But they were still after him. He couldn't rest. He had to move.

He made his way to the street. Booted feet echoed through buildings. *Where are they?* He couldn't tell. *Behind me,* he guessed. *They're coming.* The *thwoop-thwooping* of the helicopter returned, drowning out the sound of the boots. But the spotlight hadn't found him yet.

He had to disappear. It was a miracle he was alive. Now he needed to go undercover and stop Foxx. *Hide.*

Then he saw it. Across the street on the ground, a long, thin hole was just large enough for a boy to squeeze into. He had discovered a storm drain.

As he crawled in, the stench was overwhelming. He dropped into shin-deep muck and immediately threw up. Above, a spotlight flashed by. Would the soldiers hear him gagging? He must have avoided detection by seconds. Booted feet tromped above.

How long would he have to stay down here? How safe was it?

Keep moving. Keep moving. He didn't know which way to turn, so he headed away from the Texifornia Building. He trudged through muck for nearly an hour, but Charlie finally found his way back to the hideout.

Callaya jumped for joy and licked his filthy face. She sniffed the stink all over him and watched him wash. Then she curled up beside him.

Geneva. Caught. What are they doing to you right now?

He pushed the images out of his mind. *Rest. Rest so you can think again.*

He needed help.

Where could he find it?

Where?

CHAPTER 45

Geneva's entire body was on fire. She felt as if white-hot razors were cutting her insides raw.

"This is madness!" Foxx bellowed. "I *wrote* your code! I should be able to read it!" He tore boxes of circuit boards and memory chips off the shelves, hurling them to the ground in fury.

Geneva was hooked up to a Code Analyzer ten times as large and far more sophisticated than her own. Code streamed across the screen. Foxx leaned low into her face, hatred filling his eyes.

"How did you escape? What have you done to your code set? Or was it the boy? *Who is he?*"

She tried to ignore the stabbing pain. She kept her mouth shut.

"You insolent, ungrateful wretch!" *Crash!* Foxx threw another box across the room.

"Go ahead! Scan my memory. You'll only find your own lousy programming."

Foxx grabbed her face, crushing her cheeks. "You *will* talk." He stormed out of the room.

From the hallway outside, she heard McCallum's report. *Charlie got away!*

But something new bothered her. Foxx was obsessed with

finding Charlie, but he was even more concerned about Geneva's code. Why? What had she missed?

She had downloaded The Future code into a sandboxed, encrypted section of memory. She would be able to access it without Foxx's knowledge. *If I compared my own code with The Future, what would they have in common?*

The windows were dark. *I must have slept the entire day*, Charlie thought. When he tried to move, his whole body ached. He struggled up to a sitting position.

I did it, he thought. *I harnessed the Hum and did the impossible. And I survived.*

Without Geneva's laughter, he felt terribly alone.

"Well, not for long," Charlie said aloud to Callaya. "We're gonna get her back, right, puppy?" She wagged her tail. "I'm just not sure how."

Callaya hopped up and went to the corner and sniffed his bag. It was drenched in muck. She looked at him and cocked her head.

"Smart girl!" he said. "You're right! How could I have forgotten? There's a message from Geneva in there! And I haven't read it yet! Did you know that?"

Charlie pulled the VidCel and tablet out of his bag. Both had been banged up. He tried the tablet first. It squealed, then popped. The screen, spiderwebbed and broken, flashed once and winked off with a funny smell. *Great*. Now everything depended on the VidCel. *I need that message.*

Bits of the casing had fallen away completely, exposing the inside. That screen didn't look so hot, either. He could only see the white background through the shattered black glass in a few places. Most of Geneva's message was missing, but he saw a name: Jane Virtue. And part of a number.

Jane Virtue was the lady who talked about The Future.

What did Geneva want Charlie to do?

There was only one way to find out. Even though he couldn't see the entire phone number, he highlighted it all and pressed the CALL button.

* * *

Reading Geneva's code had failed, and now the firmware upgrade had failed. Impossible! Foxx had *developed* the firmware. How could the upgrade not work? How could *any* of this not work?

Geneva's error messages made no sense. Failure. Memory mismatch. Endless loops and syntax errors. *Exception: bad magic operation failed.* He kicked a chair. *Bad magic?* The system was mocking him!

These errors weren't even possible. He hadn't programmed them!

Five upgrade attempts had failed. Now Foxx would try the sixth.

Geneva's mind had been torn open. Her sense of self had been forcibly replaced, again and again. Five times now she had regained consciousness for a moment and felt as if part of reality had been carved out, leaving a gaping void. This was torture. She would rather be pummeled by Gargan.

Her processors crunched The Future, analyzing relentlessly. Her brain had no new insight, but some deep recollection was surfacing.

Suddenly, it was over. She was *present* again.

To her amazement, the firmware upgrade hadn't worked. She could still read her current rev number. Foxx howled with rage.

CHAPTER 46

The phone rang. "This is Jane," she said, and swatted the hair-dresser's hand. Was she becoming a diva? She considered apologizing, but Jane realized she didn't *have* to apologize. She was *Jane Virtue, Voice of The Future*. It was more important to *look* professional and compassionate than to *be* professional and compassionate.

In ten minutes she would go live. This was the last show in LAanges before the launch. In the morning she would travel to some of the hottest spots as she covered the largest media rollout in history.

"Miss Virtue?" a timid voice asked.

"Yes, this is Jane." Important people shouldn't have to repeat themselves.

"My name is Charles, but my friends call me Charlie, and . . ."

She cut the voice off. "Who gave you this number?"

"Uh, my friend, Geneva."

"I don't know anyone named Geneva."

"She told me to call you. We're in trouble, and we need help. It's about Mr. Foxx."

"Meaning?" She didn't have time for this nonsense.

"Miss Virtue, he's a bad man. He's what you'd call a . . . a sorcerer. He's planning something terrible. The Future is not what you think it is."

Jane had already heard her fair share of kooks, crackpots, and conspiracy theorists. But *sorcerer*?

"How did you get this number, kid? Don't say Geneva, because I don't know her. Who gave *Geneva* the number?" Some idiot at the network would lose his job tomorrow for releasing her private number.

"She got it from Gramercy Foxx. She sent me the number right before Foxx kidnapped her. His security men grabbed her, and they almost got me."

"Sure they did," she said, and she almost clicked off the phone. But then some deep, intuitive sense made her uneasy. It was the boy's truthfulness. She could hear it in his voice. After thousands of interviews, she recognized the sound.

"OK, kid. Look, I'm on the air in just a second, so I have to go. But thanks for calling. Cast in for the launch, OK?" She made a mental note to call Foxx's security guy after the broadcast. What was his name?

"But he has her! He's taken her! You don't understa —"

The line went dead.

Jane hadn't hung up on the kid. His sudden silence disturbed her. *Hmm. He's probably just a boy with an active imagination*, she thought, flipping through her notes for the show.

"Jane. This is your cue," said a voice at the door.

"I'm coming."

But she'd call the security guy anyway.

The phone made a funny purring noise and fell silent. Charlie's hand was wet. Fluid oozed all over it. Something inside had ruptured during the fall, and now it was leaking.

He tried to turn it back on. No luck. *Great. Now what?* Callaya tugged his pant leg. "What am I going to do?" He scratched behind her ears.

He had gone over the Hum code again and again in his mind. The portion that baffled both of them had matched the puppy *so* closely. Which didn't make sense. Why would Foxx need any of that to control a robot? Normal computer code would control her just fine.

Then it dawned on him. How could he have missed it? They were operating from the wrong assumptions. The code matched because it was *mind* control.

Geneva isn't a robot. She's a human.

Foxx had Geneva. She wouldn't be dismantled, only to be reassembled later for more adventures. He was going to *kill* her.

Charlie's only advantage was the Hum. To use it he had to be centered. Anger, fear, or anxiety would block it every time.

He took a few deep breaths and began to imagine how things could be. No — *would* be. That simple change in viewpoint made everything different. Now he could visualize the steps to get from where he *was* to where he *wanted* to be. He began to talk it through to Callaya.

Think positive thoughts. "I need to . . ." *Think positive thoughts.* "I am *going* to rescue Geneva. I am *going* to . . . defeat Gramercy Foxx. OK, so that's where I need to be. That's what I'm going to do. OK, no problem." *But how?*

For once, he'd give anything to see his grandfather.

Charlie felt a stab of guilt. He'd barely thought about his grandfather at all. Was the old man worried? Or did he know?

How would his grandfather deal with Foxx?

Maybe he could go get his grandfather and bring him here.

That's it! Geneva's Smasher . . .

It seemed so simple, so obvious. Except for one catch.

I don't know how to smash atoms.

"McCallum here."

"Mr. McCallum, this is Jane Virtue."

"Yes, Ms. Virtue, what can I do for you?" He hoped she hadn't noticed the skip in his voice.

"Please, call me Jane. I received the strangest call today." She described the conversation. "I know it sounds odd, but there was something so earnest about the way he said it that I believed him."

"Is this the first call where somebody has claimed Mr. Foxx is up to no good?"

She laughed. "No. You're right. People tell me that every day."

"Well, don't worry about it. But I'll follow up anyway. What did you say the boy's number was?"

Jane gave him the number from her Caller ID. McCallum recognized it — the same number that had been offline since the boy disappeared down the stairwell. That's the way they'd tracked him in the first place.

How could she have received a call from it? The boy must have known they could track him. He'd turned it off for safety. Turning it on again would re-enable calls. Clever.

"You're doing a great job out there, Jane. And good luck. You leave for the tour in the morning?"

"Yes. Thank you, John."

He called the Comm Team. The number had indeed placed a brief call earlier today, and then it had gone back offline. But now McCallum had a name: *Charlie.* He dispatched two teams and the spider-bots to search the phone's general area. *Sometimes you actually find the needle in the haystack.*

"Electricity won't hurt me, old man. Why do you bother?"

"You have outsmarted me, Geneva. Whatever you have done has proven more clever than my imperfect programming. So be it. I have other methods."

She didn't like where this was going.

He placed his manicured fingertips at her temples and closed his eyes. He began to speak the strange, soft music that connected him to the Hum.

Two months ago, Geneva would not have understood, but all that had changed. She needed to make him lose his focus.

"Seven, fourteen, ninety-eight." Random numbers always distracted her when she was concentrating. Maybe it would distract Foxx.

Foxx opened his eyes and shot her a poisonous look.

Awesome. It was working. She threw her voice around the room, whispering, then shouting. She began to sing the most irritating song she could think of. *Off-key. Loud.*

"It's your birthday! Happy birthday!"

Smack! Foxx slapped her. Then he sealed her mouth shut with duct tape.

Two minutes later, he was back in a Hum trance.

Geneva was relieved. She felt nothing. But then Foxx pulled his hands away.

Zzz-ap! She felt it all — the painful race of electricity into her ultra-capacitors, the terrible sickness as Foxx's enchantment sank into her mind, her computers, her sense of self. The Hum succeeded. *And what will happen to The Future code? Will he find it?*

But along with the electricity and the new programming came memories. Not the fragmented, confused ghosts she had lived with for so long. Geneva's memories came back *clear*. They were not complete, but they were readable.

She opened her eyes wide with shock. For the first time that she could remember, she asked herself: *Who am I?* Not *what* am I, but *Who am I?* She tried to shout, but the duct tape stifled all but a moan.

Everything in her world had changed.

CHAPTER 47

Charlie and Callaya stood in the alley where Geneva brought him from the past. To go back, he knew he had to find the exact spot.

He felt it more than he saw it — a manhole cover. To his surprise, it lifted easily. Was it the puppy? He rolled the cover away. The Hum glowed out of the hole.

Charlie was ready to go.

Geneva could barely tell the difference between the voices in the room and the voices in her head. Foxx had ravaged her programming. She could still process information, yet something was dramatically different.

She tried, but she still couldn't identify the change.

You won't find it, my love. You won't find it because it's not there.

No! Foxx had found a way into her *mind*! Now he came over and stood in front of her.

"Mmurrrrmmmm!" The duct tape still sealed her mouth.

There's no need for words. I have unlocked your memories, my love.

I'm not your love! What have you done to me?

You aren't a robot, Geneva.

Foxx waited for a reaction. He got none.

You're human. A real girl.

Liar!

Like Pinocchio. Your tech mods are advanced robotics, even for me. You were quite a challenge in surgery. Reverse engineering isn't typically done inside a living body. But modern medicine and the Hum kept you alive. I assure you that you're human: flesh and bone.

She tried to keep her expression frozen, but her eyes fluttered.

That's right, Geneva. And you will help me now. None of your plotting or scheming will change you back. Your new friend cannot save you. Your power of time travel has always been from the Hum, not from technology. And now, your technology and the Hum will help me to spread The Future. Sleep. Your accomplishments will add to mine. You should feel privileged.

Geneva's eyes closed. A white fog filled her mind while Foxx made his final preparations to enslave the entire human race.

CHAPTER 48

Charlie cursed LAanges.

He wouldn't have been able to travel through time back in Eamsford, where the flow of the Hum was strong. It was far too difficult. In this noisy, distracting time, it was impossible. *Geneva said it would be easier the second time.*

His first attempt had been exhausting. He failed completely.

His second try, he felt the pull of the Hum, but no portal had opened.

He had been counting on Callaya's help. *If only dogs could talk*, he thought, *she might be able to tell me what to do.*

This time he set Callaya between his feet. He struggled to clear his mind. Geneva hadn't done that, but she hadn't been drawing upon the power of the Hum.

Or had she?

He closed his eyes and went back in time to that day at the riverbank. What had she done? It had seemed so simple when she touched her fingers together. Effortlessly a tunnel of blue had appeared.

There was something else, though, wasn't there? Something she'd said or done that had made him think she was a student of the Hum, even though she denied it.

Believe, believe, believe . . .

Her arms in a circle, she had touched her fingers together. *Smasher.* Particles inside her accelerated in a circle around her *arms* until they *smashed* into each other. A black hole.

Fine for Geneva. But how do I do it? He focused on the part he *did* understand . . . synchronize with the Hum. Create a portal.

"Are you ready?" he asked Callaya.

She wagged her tail.

He hummed to himself, and suddenly he felt it — a slight dip, or a catch — where the polarity of the field lines aligned. His spine tingled. *There* — that was it. The Hum flowed up through the soles of his feet, through Callaya. He felt its power surge up into his arms like electrical plasma. His arms formed a circle, and he felt the flow of the Hum racing around his body faster and faster. It was time.

"Smasher."

He touched the tips of his fingers together. He closed the circuit.

Charlie could barely keep himself from being blown apart. But he held on.

Believe . . .

Believe . . .

Believe . . .

Then it happened. The air shuddered, changing from a Hum vibration into swirling, liquid energy.

Crack! A flash of light in front of him illuminated a shimmering blue portal inside the manhole.

Without hesitation, he scooped up Callaya and leaped in.

CHAPTER 49

Foxx didn't notice it at first. But then he felt the unique discomfort that could only be related to the Hum.

The girl was here, under his control. That left the boy. *What are you doing?*

Was it the puppy?

Geneva and Gargan had been his greatest achievements — until that dog. He carefully selected the breed for its loyalty and empathy. The puppy would tightly bond with its master. It would love him unconditionally. This time he used more Hum and less technology. The dog was a catalyst — to enhance Foxx's use of the Hum.

Man's best friend, he thought bitterly. But now he could neither control nor communicate with it. He'd relied on the dog's love for him as its creator. Foxx was its master until the boy stole it.

Clearly the dog could amplify the Hum for someone else. Together their power was far, far greater. The stupid boy probably had no idea.

It all brought back one of his painful memories — his twin sister again — the golden girl, so unfairly gifted. He was seven years old when he brought home a baby spaniel. The first thing his puppy did was bolt out of his arms and dash into the lap of his sister! He was too ashamed to try to pry the dog away. And his father had laughed. He thought it was cute.

Now both the boy and the dog had vanished. Where were they?

No matter, Foxx told himself. Soon he would have so much power that a nuisance like the boy would be of no consequence at all.

PART IV: SKELETONS IN THE CLOSET

CHAPTER 50

Charlie and Callaya were alone in the shimmering blue light.

The puppy adapted quickly. But Charlie was fearful. What if he and Callaya were separated? What if he couldn't find his way home?

Charlie's strength was draining. He gasped for air.

Grandfather's strong hand pulled Charlie clear.

The boy opened his eyes. He saw his grandfather's lined face and white beard. Instead of disapproval and disappointment, the old man's eyes gleamed with encouragement.

Charlie's mind's eye flashed on Geneva's face.

"Grandfather! You have to come back with me!"

"Easy, boy, easy. I know what you have to do. You will return when the time is right. Now you must come with me. You need to rest and heal."

Grandfather hoisted Charlie to his feet. "And who is this?" Grandfather asked, picking up the puppy. "Oh, you are very special. I can feel it."

Charlie looked back at the river. He didn't want Grandfather to see him cry. "I apologize. I left you," he began. "You must have been sad, and . . ."

"I know, boy. I know. You don't have to explain."

*   *   *

In the small mountain cabin, Grandfather brought him a cup of steaming tea. "You need your strength."

Callaya jumped on Charlie's lap.

The old man sat cross-legged on the floor across the room from him.

"Grandfather, I need your help. Please come to LAanges with me."

"I'm proud of you; I know it was difficult for you to ask. But I cannot do that," his grandfather said. "I have not been honest with you. An important piece of your story is missing. There isn't much time, so I will tell you now. Then you must be on your way."

"What do you mean?"

"I told you about the Interrogator. They took your father and your grandmother. Accused them of witchcraft. The rest of us fled."

"And the Interrogator killed my mother. She was trying to save the others."

"That is partly true. Charla did die at the hand of the Interrogator. But she was driven to him by her brother. Tricked. Trapped. Murdered."

"Brother? Why would he want her murdered? Was she a bad person?"

His grandfather's eyes filled with tears. "No, no — Charla was good. And talented. She was a genius, and you have never seen anyone so kind. People loved her. That can be ruinous to a brother who is not so talented, not so loved."

"It wasn't her fault she had more talent."

"True. But he grew bitter, watching doors open so easily for her when he had to struggle. Charla was kind, but she was not always kind to him. She lorded her accomplishments over him. His envy grew to hatred."

The old man blew a slow, perfectly formed smoke ring that drifted up above the fireplace. "The evil man who will . . . bring forth the plague? What is his name?"

"Gramercy Foxx."

"Hmm. Is he a young man?"

"It's hard to tell. He seems ageless. But he's cruel — he uses the Hum to do evil things. How can he do that, Grandfather? I thought the Hum was only for good."

"When a man does that, he has something deep inside he needs to prove to himself — by proving it to the world. That hatred can only have its roots in unbearable pain."

Grandfather looked off into the distance, deep in thought. "It has been many years . . . I had begun to doubt . . ."

Above the fireplace, the smoke ring condensed into a nearly solid cloud. It changed shape, and Charlie could make out a nose and then a mouth. The eyes opened. There was no mistaking it. The face of Gramercy Foxx hovered in the room.

Charlie's stomach dropped. "Grandfather, that's him!"

"Callis . . ."

"Yes! That's the name he used! How could you know that?"

"Callis is your mother's twin brother. I only hope he does not yet suspect *your* identity."

CHAPTER 51

"Ladies and gentlemen of the world, The Future . . . is just twenty-four hours away. This evening the stadium is filled to capacity. More than ninety thousand people are gathered to count down to the most monumental experience of this century."

Jane stood on a huge stage at one end of massive Crawford Soccer Stadium.

"Over the next twenty-four hours, we'll check in with cities around the world. Gramercy Foxx himself will unveil The Future, which even *I* have yet to see. But right now it's time to kick off the biggest party of the millennium. The Future is bright indeed!"

John McCallum watched Jane on the wall monitor. She was doing a great job. How could she stay calm in front of the cameras? The few times he'd been interviewed, he came across as grumpy and sour. Well, maybe he *was* grumpy and sour.

The entire building was locked down. No recycling chutes, user accounts, or elevator shafts had been left unchecked. The TerraThinc Building was secure. There would be no incidents in the next twenty-four hours.

Garcia and Molina were following up on the data collected by the spider-bots. Foxx had instructed them to monitor an anomaly from a distance.

"Be ready for anything," McCallum had said.

CHAPTER 52

Gramercy Foxx . . . his *uncle*? "Grandfather, what happened to my mother?"

"Callis tricked her. He knew her weakness — pride. He wasn't her match, but he was highly intelligent and excellent at trickery."

"What happened?"

"It was a dark, dark time, Charles. The Interrogator had come for your grandmother, and then they returned for your father. Who was next? We went into hiding. Callis wasn't even on their lists — more salt in the wound for him.

"Callis told your mother that he had bribed the guards. She would sneak in and rescue our family. He knew she'd take the bait, and she did.

"But he had really sold her to the Interrogator's men. He would be rid of his sister. They paid him for his efforts. One of his greatest gifts was for setting traps by persuading people of his truthfulness."

"So they killed her?"

"You know that part of the story, Charles."

"What happened to Callis after that?"

"Word got out about what he had done. He was shunned. Driven away."

"To the future? But how did he do it? He's never been able to time travel again. My friend thinks he's stuck."

"*He* didn't do it. Your mother did. Charla was proud — and she bragged to him that she had learned how to open a Resonant Gap, a void in the Hum. Callis merely had to persuade her to keep the portal open. We were being hunted like animals. Keeping it open allowed an escape route."

"So he escaped to the future?"

"All I saw was a flash. Then he was gone."

"Smasher," Charlie said softly.

"What's that?"

"My friend Geneva learned how to time travel. She smashes atoms together."

"Atoms? You've learned a lot in the future. Is that how you came back?"

"I reopened a portal that was already there. And I had a little help," Charlie added, ruffling Callaya's head. "But please, Grandfather, tell me the rest."

"There's nothing left to tell. The coward fled. He entered the portal the morning the Interrogator put them to death."

"Why didn't you tell me?"

"I should have, but I didn't want to burden you with such a tale."

Charlie felt a burst of anger. "You should have told me the truth!" Callaya jumped off his lap.

"You lack the years to understand what it means to helplessly stand by as those you love are taken from you and murdered in cold blood. And you will *not* raise your voice to me."

Charlie locked eyes with his grandfather. For the first time, he didn't back down.

A high-pitched snarl distracted both of them. Callaya crouched low between Charlie's feet and growled at his grandfather. The old man laughed.

"Please call off your brave protector," Grandfather said.

Charlie exhaled slowly. "I'm going back tomorrow. Somebody has to stop Foxx. You could come, you know. After all, he's your *son*."

"I can't help," Grandfather said with finality. "Look at me. I'm an old man, Charles. I'd like to say I'd kill him for what he did, but in truth, he would certainly kill me. As he may kill you. But I won't stop you."

"But how can I stop *him*?"

"Callis will fall, Charles, because he *must*. His actions are selfish. He *cannot* succeed. You will find his mistake, his weakness, and you will exploit it."

What weakness could there be?

"If he's so evil," Charlie began, "how can he be so powerful? You always say that in order to connect to the Hum, I have to keep love in my heart."

"Love comes in many forms, Charles. I would not presume to grasp them all, nor should you." He paused, weighing how best to continue. "I truly believe that love is necessary. Since I believe it, then it is absolutely necessary . . . *for me*. I cannot feel the Hum without love. But there are those who do not believe that."

Before Charlie could answer, the old man reached forward and touched Charlie's eyes. Suddenly Charlie was exhausted.

"No more questions. Now is the time for *rest*. Then you will go back to do what you must."

Charlie lay down on his little bed. Within minutes he was sound asleep with Callaya in his arms.

CHAPTER 53

Charlie sat bolt upright. "I have to get back."

Grandfather's voice startled him. "You will, my boy. But I have a gift for you. The first thing the evil ones steal is hope." Grandfather held out a dark wooden box. "Pandora's Box," he said, one eyebrow cocked.

Charlie knew the myth — how Pandora opened a forbidden box. To her horror, all the evils in the world rushed out. Afterward, one small thing had remained inside the box: hope.

"It's a trap, Charles. A *Hum* trap. It would be nice if Pandora could put a little of the world's evil back into the box, don't you agree?" The box was surprisingly light. "It will feel the proper weight when it holds its intended captive."

"Callis?"

"I wanted to stop him. If Callis is near the open box, it will capture him."

Grandfather opened a second box. Inside was a row of small vials — family blood, kept fresh in an enchanted box. Grandfather held up a nearly empty vial — the blood of Callis. He had used it to create Pandora's Box.

"When I first completed the box, I opened it, hoping it would draw him back. It did not work, but the box proved its power — it nearly sucked *me* in. Sensing the same blood in my veins, it would settle for me. It took all my strength to close it. Do not open it until you are near him! It may like you nearly as much as it likes him."

"You didn't make this with love in your heart, did you?"

"I made it with love for your mother and grandmother."

Charlie carefully placed Pandora's Box in a leather pack his grandfather had made to carry it. Then he picked up his puppy.

"Before you go . . . your dog . . . she's very powerful. But you know that already, don't you?"

"She's already saved my life at least once."

"She may yet again." Grandfather escorted Charlie to the door. "She will make things possible that you never imagined. If she likes you, that is." Grandfather shot Charlie a rare, wry smile.

"Are there other dogs like her?" Charlie asked.

"Not that I've seen. Where did you find her?"

"Foxx made her — enhanced her, I mean. And I took her away."

"Ahhh. That explains it. She's much better off in your care, I'm sure. He was never kind to animals. They sensed that and stayed away. But hurry, now. You must go."

His grandfather had never been a person to hug, but today Charlie embraced him anyway, hoping it would not be the last time.

The puppy looked at the old man and barked.

Charlie patted her head. "What's up, Callaya?"

Grandfather looked stricken.

"She doesn't mean any harm by it," Charlie said.

"Is that her name? Callaya?"

"It is. I made the name up. Why? Don't you like it?"

"That was your mother's name, when she was born. . . ."

"And you changed it to Charla? And then named me Charles, after her?"

"We gave her a safe name the priests wouldn't question. It was your grandmother's idea, and it was a good one. How peculiar that you remembered. But now you and Callaya . . . you need to go."

Charlie took her out into the nighttime air.

"One more thing, Charles," Grandfather called after him. "Happy birthday."

Charlie hadn't even thought about that. He shot a tired smile back at the old man. "Thanks for remembering."

As he walked down the hill toward the stream, he absently wondered if it would still be his birthday when he got to LAanges.

CHAPTER 54

Two more men had been assigned to the stakeout, so Garcia and Molina ventured down to the manhole for a closer look. They saw the strange glowing water, and Molina made a crack about guarding a toilet. Garcia didn't find it funny.

Garcia went to the roof of a parking structure for an angle. McCallum contacted street maintenance to make sure they didn't replace the manhole cover. McCallum wanted the site untouched so the kid wouldn't get spooked if he turned up. Molina continued with the toilet jokes until Garcia told him to shut up. "We missed the kid once. I don't want it to happen again."

"Come on," Molina griped. "A glowing toilet? Weird, right?"

Garcia sent one of the rent-a-cops down another manhole, underground, to watch the glowing river from below. He was a skinny kid with red hair and freckles who insisted on being called Lazer.

"What's your status?"

"Zero activity in the bird's nest, sir," Garcia replied. "Molina is on the ground, Ramirez is in the car, and Lazer is in the sewer. Sir, he's thrown up twice already."

"Well, stay on it. T minus eight hours. No time for screw-ups. McCallum out." It would have been a lot nicer to handle the security detail escorting Jane Virtue from the airport to Foxx's office. "You can't win 'em all, Johnny boy," he chided himself.

CHAPTER 55

The tiniest sliver of light hovered above the river where the portal had been. *Geneva,* Charlie thought. *I wish you were here.*

Charlie half slid, half walked down the muddy bank. He was on his own now. There would be no one in LAanges to rescue him.

All around him, the sensation of the Hum was so strong! It washed into him in huge waves . . . so plentiful, so effortless. He placed Callaya between his feet. Then he made a circle with his arms and put his fingertips together.

Smasher.

A flash of light lit the darkness around him. The portal opened wide. It was time to go.

Once inside, he released Callaya and opened his eyes.

He kicked forward. *Smasher. Wow.*

Callaya paddled a few feet behind him. He scooped her up again. He could swear the puppy was smiling.

Now he had to find the right exit among the thousands of tiny white points.

Trust your intuition. You know. Believe.

He did.

Each kick propelled him straight as an arrow across the void until he was peering sideways through a round hole of blue sky. *LAanges*. This time exiting was easy.

The hard part would be getting out of the open manhole. With Pandora's Box in the pouch on his back and Callaya tucked in the crook of his arm, Charlie wrestled his way up until he could see the edge of the street.

Screech! A car swerved past. Charlie ducked.

CHAPTER 56

Garcia saw a slight movement out of the corner of his eye. Instead of watching the site, he'd been watching a gorgeous girl in a short skirt. Had he missed something? He checked the Digiscope. Nothing. A driver probably tossed something out a car window. He rolled the recording back. His radio beeped. Molina.

"Did you see those long legs? Hotty hot hotness."

"Yeah, yeah. Knock it off. Did you notice anything at the hole a second ago? I'm checking playback now. What the —?"

There it was — a moving shadow. Garcia hit ENHANCE. That was no shadow. It was the top of a head.

Instead of risking the cars, Charlie went back down into the portal and exited into the sewer. He descended the ladder and hoped he would find a safer exit.

But a voice shouted at him from below. "Freeze!" It was a skinny, redheaded kid who looked way too young to be yelling orders. Except for one thing.

He had a gun.

"I said *f-f-freeze*! D-d-don't move!" His voice was shaking. The kid hit a button on his helmet. "Garcia! I've got him. He ain't goin' nowhere with Lazer on the scene."

Charlie couldn't believe he was about to get caught by a complete loser. He had escaped Foxx's security squad. He had survived Gargan. He had traveled through time. Surely he could handle this. He gritted his teeth and aimed as he stepped off the ladder. He dropped ten feet like a bag of cement.

Lazer flinched, trying to get out of the way. His finger instinctively pulled the trigger.

Bang! The bullet bounced harmlessly off concrete.

Charlie's feet slammed into Lazer's raised arms. The gun rammed Lazer's chin, and he crumpled into the muck. Charlie landed on top of him, Callaya still in his arms.

The rent-a-cop was out cold, his bloody face smashed against concrete.

Charlie stood up and vomited. Hard. He was in the sewer system. His last underground adventure had been in the storm drain system, where filthy water and garbage from the street drained into the ocean, but the *sewer* was the destination for all plumbing in the city — including toilets. Charlie was wading through human excrement pungent enough to make him puke again before he could even wipe his mouth.

Perfect. Just perfect.

The redhead would live, so Charlie took off. More armed guards would be there any minute.

"Lazer? Lazer?" No answer. "Come in, McGillicutty — you rent-a-cop!" Still nothing. Garcia keyed the team channel. "Ramirez, Molina! Get down there. Something happened to that imbecile. Don't let the boy get away!"

Garcia redeployed sensor bots to the manhole to scan for signs of life belowground. McCallum wouldn't be happy.

Garcia was right. "Do *not* let him get away!" McCallum roared from his office at TerraThine. Once again he was amazed at the courage of the boy, but the blunders of his team were highly embarrassing. The boy had chosen to surface again. He gave McCallum no choice.

"Molina here. Going down the manhole, sir. McGillicutty's alive but injured."

"Ramirez, what's your location?"

"Underground a block away, sir! What's the lay of the land?"

"The manhole is about five hundred yards north of a major line crossing. Do not let the kid get to that intersection!" *What did the boy do to McGillicutty? Lazer was just a know-nothing rent-a-cop, but still . . .*

Charlie was running as fast as he could in the filthy, slippery stench. How did they find him so fast?

He slipped in a slime patch. Callaya dropped into the muck. Cursing, Charlie scrambled back to his feet. He scooped up Callaya, trying not to inhale.

Less than a minute later, they came to an intersection. He had no idea which way to go. Six tunnels converged and drained to a lower level. Frantically he looked into one tunnel after another — and then he lost track of where he came from.

Panic.

Pay attention to the puppy. He gently put her down into the muck. "Which way, girl? Come on. Show me the way."

Callaya pushed her way to the left. Sewage rose nearly to her shoulders. She slid to a stop in front of one tunnel.

She sniffed, then plowed down the tunnel, barely glancing back at him.

Charlie followed.

Spider-bots returned data as they spread across the neighborhood. So far, they'd tracked Ramirez and Molina. But they still didn't have a lead on the kid. Ramirez was now deep down in the sewer. Garcia fed him directions.

Molina had brought up McGillicutty, who was on the way to the hospital. Now Molina was tracking on foot again. When he reached the main crossing empty-handed, Garcia told him to hold. "Wait for the bots to find the kid."

Something felt wrong. What was it? McCallum had always trusted his instincts before, and he sensed something unusual here . . . something of greater significance.

He had been revolted by what Foxx was doing to Geneva. Robot or not, McCallum knew pain when he saw it. And now the boy was on the run again. Surely Foxx would torture him, too. They were children — determined children on a mission. But what was it? What did they know that made Gramercy Foxx so uneasy?

This kid was important. Foxx stressed they must capture him. McCallum worked for Foxx because Foxx was considered a great man. Serving such a distinguished man was an opportunity not to be squandered. A thousand qualified men would love to snatch McCallum's job. But something was off.

Enough. The instincts lose today. Keep your job. Don't overthink it.

"Sir, we're holding for the sensor bots to give us a lead," Garcia said. "We don't have the manpower to chase this kid through the sewers, sir."

"Fine. Backup is on the way with two more cases of spiders. You have tactical authority. McCallum out." He blinked, trying to shake a growing headache. He watched the data, calculating how to capture the most elusive kid ever.

Callaya had stopped around a corner, chest-deep in filth. She wagged her tail and looked up at Charlie happily. A dead end.

If they got caught here, it was all over. The ceiling was smooth — no manhole, no ladder, no escape. Charlie listened for splashing feet. But all he heard was the gurgling of sewage.

They would have to double back.

That turned out to be easy enough; he found another manhole not far behind. But climbing up the ladder was treacherous. His sewage-covered feet kept slipping. Then there was the problem of the manhole cover. Prying it from above was one thing. From below . . . *How did Geneva lift it the first time? Right. She was a robot.*

The other exits would be the same. He had to get out.

He tucked Callaya into his shirt. Climbing was easier. He could see sunlight through the holes in the cover. A shadow passed over, eclipsing one hole at a time. It was something small.

Charlie climbed up to look through a hole. That one blacked out, too, until his eye adjusted.

A shiny silver bug stared back at him.

"Ouch!" It nearly jabbed him in the eye! He stepped down a rung as it crawled through the hole and hung there . . . watching him.

He froze. It was a tiny robot spider! Unbelievable!

Then another bug crawled through. He recoiled. Now another. In a few seconds, half a dozen crawled through.

Foxx had found him.

"We've got him, sir!" Garcia shouted. "I'm staring the kid in the face, sir — the bugs have him!" A fish-eye video of Charlie's face filled Garcia's screen.

"Get your men moving!" McCallum bellowed.

"Already rolling, sir." Garcia slammed the brakes to avoid ramming a garbage truck. "I'll be at their position in less than three minutes, sir. They are stationary and belowground."

"Do *not* let him get away this time."

Garcia would never allow it. He had two teams bearing down on a *boy*. They'd capture him for sure.

Charlie hated spiders. He closed his eyes to block out the swarm of bots. They were crawling *on* him now. Knowing they were robots offered little comfort. He was covered in sewage, lost and trapped in an underground maze, and an army of guards was on the way. How much worse could it get?

The Hum, he thought. He had tried to levitate an object this heavy once before — under his grandfather's supervision. He'd failed. But now he had the puppy.

Believe, he told himself once again. Could he do it?

Believe, or don't even try.

Charlie ignored the revolting spiders crawling into his shirt. He focused on raising the cover. The Hum tingled in his feet, and then he felt a strong flow in the tips of his fingers where he touched Callaya.

The Hum began to fill him up, swirling around him, invisible to the human eye. But the other eyes focused on Charlie were not human. They recorded a change in the electroweak currents, and they reported back. When the manhole cover floated away, the spider-bots set off an alarm on McCallum's screen. They also sent an alarm to the desk of Gramercy Foxx himself.

McCallum jumped when the Foxx light came on. "Yes, sir, I see it."

"Those are *my* sensors," Foxx hissed from two hundred stories above. "They report to me."

"Yes, sir."

"I am seven hours away from the most important event in history. I do not have time for this. Find the boy. Bring him to me. Do not make me find him myself."

"As you command, sir! I will find the boy. He will be stopped!"

"Good." The intercom clicked off.

McCallum caught his breath and realized he was standing at attention. Why was his face wet? Had he been crying? He felt light-headed but clear about his orders. He leaped into action.

"Blue Bird, Blue Bird, what's your status?"

"Blue Bird here. Landing on the roof of the parking structure now, sir. Will come across the bridge on the 25th floor. Headed for the helipad on the main building."

"I'll meet you there." He grabbed his Mark V on his way through the bullpen. This kid would *not* get the best of him again.

Charlie shook the last spiders off, glad they didn't bite. He and Callaya were in the alley by the hideout. When the puppy had stopped in the sewer line and wagged her tail, they had been directly under the building. Amazing.

By now the men chasing him must have pinpointed his exact location — and that meant the hideout. But he didn't know where else to go.

Screech! In the street at the far end of the alley, a large black vehicle sped toward Charlie. A heavily armed man on foot rounded the corner at the other end.

Trapped! Charlie twisted hard for the dumbwaiter but lost his footing. He barely managed to keep from falling.

"Get him!" Garcia shouted to Molina over the truck radio. The truck jolted across the potholes between him and the boy.

Molina was halfway down the alley.

"Sir, I have the kid cornered."

"Do *not* let him get away."

Garcia slammed on the brakes. Dust erupted from the worn pavement and gravel — he'd stopped the truck much too close.

Charlie dove behind a Dumpster. He heaved the dumbwaiter door open and threw Callaya in. He tried to jump after her, but the leather pouch snagged on the door. Wild with panic, he slid out to try again.

Molina was just behind on foot. But the truck's dust cloud cut off his view.

Charlie leaped with all his strength. He heaved himself

forward, and his legs cleared the opening. The metal door closed halfway, and the dumbwaiter inched upward.

Molina was furious. The kid's feet were disappearing behind the metal door! He dove. His shoulder rammed into the brick wall, but he had the kid's foot.

Pain shot up Charlie's leg. He flipped over. One of the security guys had him. Charlie grabbed the dumbwaiter rope for leverage and pulled up. With the sudden strength of pure rage, Charlie kicked his free heel straight down, rodeo style.

Molina's head snapped back. He was unconscious before he hit the ground.

Garcia saw it in slow motion. He hoped Molina's neck wasn't broken.

The metal door clanged shut. By the time Garcia wrenched it open, the kid had raised the dumbwaiter just out of reach.

Garcia leaned in and grabbed the rope. The dumbwaiter stopped. After a few seconds' tug-of-war, the box suddenly reversed. *Screek!* Down it came —*fast*. Garcia dove back, barely making it out alive. *The kid tried to crush me!*

Now the dumbwaiter cranked back up. Garcia looked over at Molina. He was stretched out on the pavement, moaning but alive. Unbelievably, the kid had managed to escape again.

CHAPTER 57

Charlie wedged a bench into the open dumbwaiter. The security goons could pull all day, and it wouldn't get them anywhere.

Then the spiders started crawling in the open window. Charlie closed it tight and scrambled after them, crushing each one with a paint can. Callaya pounced and bit a bug's head off, but the electrical shock made her yelp.

Charlie rinsed himself off, changed clothes, and washed Callaya. Then he collapsed against the wall. If only he and his puppy could slip away. Foxx could have his mind-control virus and run the world.

But Foxx had Geneva. And he would not get away with murder again.

Charlie had work to do. The Future was his own family's hideous creation. It was his *responsibility* to destroy it.

Big words, but now what? Charlie was trapped, surrounded, and alone.

"Garcia, do you have the target?"

"That's a negative, sir. He's inside. Guards are covering the exits."

McCallum hovered overhead in Blue Bird. This was the very neighborhood where he had flown Foxx.

Charlie hugged his knees. The helicopter grew louder, then faded away. A voice boomed, "Come out! You're surrounded!"

What will happen when they take me? They wouldn't kill him. They were working too hard to catch him.

By now, Geneva was no doubt dead. Did Foxx know she'd inserted a code into The Future? And did he know she'd sent Charlie that code? What would it do?

What *would* it do?

His mind snapped to attention. Her code was still on the broken cell phone, and he had the Code Analyzer!

Shutting out all the banging and shouting, Charlie connected the phone to the analyzer and launched the sequence.

The analyzer was able to pull Geneva's codes directly out of the memory chips. Charlie had learned a *lot* about computers. But when the Code Analyzer told him he was looking at a Nested Port/Time-Variable, Spread Spectrum Firewall Exploit, it didn't mean a thing to him — it was too advanced. Same with the code Geneva inserted into The Future.

The last piece of code was an excerpt from The Future — the code that closely matched that of Geneva and Callaya.

Two minutes of translation later he understood. Part of the code converted three different types of energy into Hum energy — electrical, potential, spiritual. Geneva's code referenced electrical energy to be able to time travel. Callaya's code referenced potential energy, which made sense because she was a catalyst. And The Future referenced spiritual energy. Spiritual energy? Belief itself? Life force? That sounded insane. Charlie was completely confused. What would Foxx do with *that*?

The sensor bots couldn't actually see him. But infrared read-outs showed Charlie through the walls.

"Let's see," McCallum growled.

Garcia spun out an image of the building. "He's been sitting right there, but now he's moving." Garcia pointed out a red and yellow rectangle. "There must be a powerful piece of hardware in there."

"Watch him. And let me know when demolition gets here. We're going in."

Charlie set Callaya in his lap and closed his eyes. He hummed the notes he used to do his homework back home. The music gave him an edge, especially when he studied math. Maybe it would help here.

It did.

Geneva had opened a back door to Foxx's network that was very difficult to detect. Charlie didn't know how to take advantage of it — with or without the Hum.

Brainstorming time. What could he put in the back door? Geneva had taught him about computer viruses; The Future code was a virus. But Charlie couldn't *write* one. Once upon a time, viruses spread through email. Then viruses were replaced by stuff that was even worse — worms, Trojans, spyware, root kits, malware.

Boom! Boom! The military types were on the roof now.

What could Charlie do? Now that he had Pandora's Box, was there a way to get it into TerraThinc? A back door couldn't get it in there, could it?

Wait.

What if the back door could get *him* inside with the box?

He had once transmogrified a pebble into a flower. He wished he could just turn himself into a bird and fly off. He couldn't do that, but he did know how to translate the Hum code and DNA code. It was an insanely difficult idea, but could he transmogrify himself into the computer? The Future code was based on DNA, which defined a person or an animal, so why couldn't he transmogrify himself into a code — The Charlie Code? He could send himself into that back door if he were a code, couldn't he?

Except . . . he had no idea how to do that.

But Callaya would help. As Grandfather pointed out, Callaya was a catalyst. She'd enhance any connection he made with the Hum. The Hum required belief — so if he *believed*, could he send himself into that back door?

Maybe he'd fail and get caught.

Maybe it would work.

Above him, plaster dust began snowing down from the ceiling. Somebody was drilling up there. Time was running out.

Maybe it would get him out of this building, where he was surrounded. That alone made it worth a try.

Did he have a better idea? No.

First, he needed to be sure he could actually get in there. He put the Code Analyzer into Security mode. Geneva had already set it up, so Charlie just hit the button. The TerraThinc IP6 addresses appeared. The system scanned *everything*, but each scan returned *nothing*. The entire building had been locked down.

Only the most critical information got through. A handful

of websites and email addresses worked. Gfoxx1@terrathinc. com was accepting email. That must be Foxx's new address. The old ones didn't work.

What if he emailed himself to Foxx? Email could go through. He could transmogrify into digital information — into energy — and email himself to Foxx! It was wild, but it wasn't impossible. When Foxx opened the email, Charlie would turn back into himself, trap Foxx in Pandora's Box, and save the day! Simple!

Ha! Simple. Right. There was nothing simple about it.

Next: How to transmogrify? Only a true master could transform out of his body. Grandfather could do it. He once turned into a wolf and chased a prowler up a tree. But that was Grandfather. Still, Charlie had Callaya. She'd worked wonders so far.

Charlie wanted to change into an email — a *code*. His DNA identified *him*. Turn his *DNA* code into *digital* code. Convert his physical self into intangible information — into *energy*.

This was his craziest idea yet.

But it was the Hum, not engineering.

He thought of Grandfather's mathematical proofs. *The Hum is a relationship between matter and energy,* and *I am able to manipulate the Hum,* therefore *I am able to manipulate energy,* therefore *I can turn matter into energy.*

This will never work.

Intention and belief, he reminded himself. His hands were already shaking.

Callaya would sit in his lap with the box, and then they'd be . . . *digital.* But where would they go? *We'll go into the computer.* He connected it to the Code Analyzer.

Another problem was size: DNA was a *very* long molecule. Stretched out, a single molecule would be three feet long. But every cell's DNA twisted on itself until it crammed into the cell nucleus.

Charlie needed to turn *all* of himself into digital information. He couldn't miss a single part. That would be a lot of information — would he fit into the computer, into an email?

It was the Hum, not engineering.

He didn't need to *understand*. He needed to *believe*. The Hum could compress more powerfully than anything a computer scientist could develop.

Intention and belief, intention and belief.

Once he had gone digital and had made it into the computer, he'd need to get to Foxx. Charlie Email would have to get past firewalls and antivirus protection, but most important, Foxx would have to open it. If Foxx didn't open the email, then there was no point. Charlie could end up stuck forever. *Gulp.*

But Geneva had risked her life. So had Charlie's mother. He took a deep breath and began to type the email that would propel him into Foxx's network.

These days, it took a revolutionary approach to get through powerful computer defenses. Foxx was counting on it: Security software wouldn't expect The Future virus. By the same token, Foxx's defenses wouldn't expect a Charlie Code. *Intention and belief, intention and belief.*

Next up: How to get Foxx to open the email. Would he even notice it? Then would he open it? Would he open the Charlie Code attachment?

Virus writers tricked people into opening viruses by making them sound fun. "Click here for the coolest game ever!" Careful people knew not to open unexpected attachments. Gramercy Foxx was very, *very* careful. Charlie needed to out-fox Foxx.

FROM: GENEVA@TERRATHINC.COM
TO: GFOXX1@TERRATHINC.COM
SUBJECT: Callis, I Know You're Trying to Find Me
BODY: I know who you are, Callis. I know where you're from. And I know WHEN you're from. Time traveler.

Here's something your sister knew about the Hum. Read it before you release The Future.

SIGNED: The Boy Who Has Escaped You
ATTACHMENT: What You Don't Know

Between Geneva's email address and Charlie's taunt, Foxx would open it for sure. No one else could know he was from the past. And how many people knew about the Hum? It would work. It had to.

Intention and belief. Believe, believe, believe.

Charlie hadn't noticed the two tiny cameras in the ceiling that had slid in through a pair of fresh holes. They were hair-thin fiber-optic cameras that could drill with laser light as easily as they could take in the room's light to capture video.

The cameras delivered a decent 3D image. The boy had electronic contraptions spread out on a table. The puppy was on his lap.

"What's he up to?" McCallum wondered. "What's in that wooden box?"

"Food?" Garcia guessed, twisting the image to zoom, pan, and tilt.

"It's more important than that. Watch him," McCallum ordered. "Keep me posted. What's the holdup with the demolition team?"

"Traffic, sir. It ain't easy to get into downtown today."

"Figures," McCallum grunted. Traffic was bad already, but The Future had generated a mania he'd never seen before. "Let me know when they arrive."

Foxx's wireless earpiece chimed.

"We have video."

"Send me the link," Foxx snapped.

"You already have it, sir."

Foxx pulled his pen phone out of his pocket, unrolling the screen. He opened the link. The boy was hunched over a table, pulling wires on some contraption.

"We cut power to the building and it had no effect. They must be powered by the city mains. So we're waiting on demo, sir."

"There's no time." Foxx dropped the line. He spun to the table where Geneva had been strapped for a day and a half. He shoved the screen at her.

Geneva's eyes were dim. Her breathing was shallow. Foxx didn't care. "Tell me what the boy is doing, and I'll let him live."

Geneva could barely focus. Charlie was at the Code Analyzer with the dog and . . . something else. "He's . . . he's . . . in a room."

"That's right," Foxx soothed. "What is he doing? Tell me. I can stop the pain."

She didn't know. But she couldn't let Foxx see that. She had to keep him guessing. She opened her mouth as though she would spill her guts. Then she closed her mouth again and glared. Hopefully Foxx would take the bait.

"Tell me, you stupid, *stupid* girl, or the boy will feel such pain he will wish to die to end it!" Geneva gave no reaction whatsoever. Foxx pressed the button on his earpiece. "Bring the boy to me. Dead or alive — it makes no difference."

McCallum surveyed the scene. Red Team perimeter was one block out, and LAanges Police blockaded at two. No one in or out. Sensor bots swarmed the building, even in the sewer lines. The kid couldn't possibly get away.

Five hours until The Future was released. They could wait on demo for ten minutes. He had tactical command. But he cringed at the thought of disobeying his master.

Master? Something was very wrong. His head spun.

When McCallum doubled over, Garcia dashed up and pulled him to his feet. McCallum was dead weight — he dropped to his knees and vomited.

"Boss, you all right?" Garcia asked. "You've been a little . . . *off* the last few days."

"Where's the demo team?" McCallum asked, wiping his face with the back of his arm. He steadied himself on Garcia's shoulder.

"Still a few minutes out. Are you OK, sir?"

"Yeah, yeah." McCallum shook his head — too slowly. Things were getting weirder by the second. He felt drunk. But he hadn't touched a drop in four years.

McCallum craned back to look up at the helicopter, and that was it. His eyes rolled up, and his knees buckled.

Charlie ignored the voice outside. He was busy. He clipped two leads from the analyzer to his pinkies, two more to his big toes. It just seemed right. He had to go with his instincts.

Breathing correctly, he focused his mind. His feet tingled. The Hum was flowing, all right. Callaya made all the difference.

Delicate music floated in his head. He stayed out of the way — let the Hum do the work. He calmly listened as it softly poured out of him.

Callaya's head cocked to one side as she listened, too — the subtle sound of the Hum stream grew stronger and stronger.

"Sir?"

A blurry haze — someone's face was too close to McCallum's. He pushed Garcia away.

"Demo team?" he asked groggily.

"The building's wired, sir. The teams are ready. Thirty-second countdown." Garcia was looking at him with . . . ugh, pity.

"This is McCallum, resuming command. Status report." Fifteen seconds and counting.

Why had he collapsed? It was a privilege to serve a great man like Gramercy Foxx.

Foxx, a great man? He didn't remember feeling that way before. He seemed to recall wanting to resign. Ugh. The dizziness returned.

"Three, two, one . . ." came the countdown.

"All teams are go."

*   *   *

Charlie and Callaya worked together effortlessly. Charlie called the Hum, and Callaya increased the stream. The more Hum power came, the more they drew. The stream became a flood. Callaya was physically separate, but within the Hum, the boy and the dog melted together as one.

Transmogrify. It changed the very nature of matter — from a beetle to a mouse, a frog to an eagle. It made no difference — matter simply *changed* from one state to another. Now Charlie wanted to turn from a human — *matter* — into information — *energy*.

Albert Einstein determined the relationship of matter to energy. $E=MC^2$. A little bit of mass equaled an unbelievably huge amount of energy.

But this was the Hum.

It swirled around Charlie, breaking his body down, DNA strand by DNA strand, atom by atom. He and Callaya and the box were being converted into energy, into information itself.

Outside, everything went wrong.

First, seconds after the demo team leader pressed the detonation button, there should have been only a gaping hole in the side of the building. The outside wall of the hideout should have disintegrated in a brief plume of smoke.

Second, the Red Team should have poured in — men from the roof; jet bikes from the alley; and a stun cannon set to deliver a knockout electrical shock.

That was what *should* have happened. But it all relied on electricity. Charlie's use of the Hum had already energized and ionized the room. Outside, the electrical equipment would be unstable.

The electrical relays in the explosives fired imprecisely. The wall didn't shatter or pulverize. It splintered. The Hum field in the room repelled the debris and blew the wall *out*. It pummeled everyone on the ground as if a bomb had hit. Dozens would go to the hospital.

The cannon backfired, stunning the operator.

Fortunately the fuel tanks in the jet bikes didn't explode, or everyone on the roof would have been killed.

McCallum looked at his covert video screen. The boy was still sitting there with the puppy in his lap. He hadn't moved a muscle despite the explosion.

What in the world was going on? Then it got even more impossible.

Before John's eyes, the boy and the puppy began to disappear. Was it the video? The rest of the image stayed intact. No, it wasn't the video.

He couldn't give an order to move in. No one could move. Garcia was down.

It was up to McCallum. He grabbed his Mark V and leaped onto the garbage bin. Then he climbed up to the fresh hole in the wall.

The boy sat just above him, holding the puppy and a box. His eyes were closed. He continued to simply . . . *vanish*. His face and hands were dissolving away as if he'd been doused in acid.

John heaved himself in. Where seconds ago the boy and the puppy had been sitting, now there was only an empty chair.

The boy's eyes had disappeared last. Just before they vanished, they opened and looked straight at him. John wanted to crawl out of his skin.

"What," he gasped, "is happening here?"

CHAPTER 58

Charlie didn't hear the explosion. His ears were gone. The Hum was rearranging him at the molecular level. His consciousness, or spirit, floated upward, while his body, transformed into energy — information — an email attachment.

He felt his spirit float away, vaguely aware that John McCallum was climbing up. By the time McCallum shouted to cut the power to the building, Charlie, his puppy, and Pandora's Box had no physical form.

Charlie felt a spinning pressure, as if he had a head cold. His body had transformed into Charlie Email. The puppy and Pandora's Box had merged into him. He flashed down the building's InterNext connection as electrons. Then he zoomed to the high-speed routers in downtown LAanges.

Data connections were fast — blindingly fast after the last-minute upgrades. Highly compressed, Charlie Email traversed the InterNext very quickly.

Once Charlie Email was accepted, the email servers waited patiently for the complete attachment to arrive. Standard filters checked the sender, and geneva@terrathinc.com registered through TerraThinc security, bypassing much of the antivirus and antispam measures applied to less trusted sources.

Layers of security to catch unacceptable attachments failed to stop him.

From transmogrification to arrival in Foxx's mailbox, only twelve seconds passed. Charlie's consciousness followed his electrical body. Now he could only wait for the email to be opened to release him.

Inside Foxx's office, Charlie's spirit floated fifty feet or so from the vacant desk. Where was Foxx? He could *feel* Callaya, but only as an enhancer within his altered form.

He explored, visiting the 198th floor. He wasn't prepared for what he found.

Geneva was alive, strapped to a table. A large electrical harness hooked into each arm. The stripped-back nano-skin below her elbow exposed the underlying robotics. She was in agony.

Lawrence Yates adjusted electrodes and data connectors protruding from her head and chest. Foxx supervised from nearby.

Charlie's plan had to work, or she would die. He tried to reach out to her, but with no physical body he couldn't speak. He was a bubble of conscious energy.

Geneva sensed something. She opened her eyes. A presence she couldn't identify granted her a brief distraction from the pain and blinding dehydration.

But the respite couldn't last. She closed her eyes and shuddered.

Today would be the best day in Gramercy Foxx's life. *The Future is upon us! I will launch the greatest coup in the history of the world!*

Foxx stopped. It was little more than a blip on the radar, but he felt something there in the room with them, like a ghost. He closed his eyes. He could feel the Hum, but beyond that, he saw nothing, sensed nothing. Whatever it was had gone.

He wondered if today's pressure was getting to him. Yates waited, zombielike, for his next instruction. Foxx felt distracted, exasperated.

"Run them again. I want the full range of possibilities. How much will the data congestion slow us down? I'll be at my desk." He had reports to review. The release of The Future would be perfect. Everything was coming together as planned . . . with one exception.

Ambulances were on the way. Blue Bird was flying the badly injured men to the nearest hospital. McCallum had to let Foxx know what had happened.

But what *had* happened? He couldn't make sense of it. The boy was surrounded, hooked up to a machine. Somehow he had disrupted the explosives, and in the process, he'd managed to . . . what? Evaporate?

McCallum remembered the boy's disappearance in the stairwell. Was this the same thing?

He took a deep breath and hit the button for Foxx's direct line.

Charlie had returned to Foxx's office for fear of being sensed.

Foxx stormed in, shouting into his earpiece. Frustrated with his disembodied deafness, Charlie focused on the vibrating air and discovered he could hear.

"Bring me *everything*, McCallum! I want to see it all!" Foxx commanded.

The desk phone buzzed.

"What, Evelyn?"

"Miss Virtue is in the helicopter on the way here."

"Tell me when she arrives." He skimmed his email.

Charlie read over his shoulder. The subject lines all involved The Future.

Except one. A sharp breath told Charlie that Foxx had found it.

Foxx's hand almost trembled over the touch screen. Was Gramercy Foxx afraid? Then the hesitation was gone. Foxx tapped the touch screen. A message sounded about virus scanning.

Would Charlie be found out now?

The software recognized no virus.

Foxx tapped the email open.

Charlie was safe.

Foxx's eyes widened as he read the email. He sat back in his chair, reading it a second time. Then the attachment lit up — Foxx selected it, but he didn't open it. A different antivirus window appeared, scanning with more powerful software.

Charlie prepared himself. He ran over the steps. As soon as Foxx opened the attachment, Charlie would transmogrify and open Pandora's Box. Foxx would be captured and powerless to launch The Future. The world would be safe.

But Foxx didn't open the attachment. Why not?

Open it! Charlie wanted to scream.

Foxx abruptly spun in his chair and stood up, staring at Charlie's presence. Foxx knew! An eternity passed until Charlie realized Foxx wasn't looking *at* him, but *through* him. The man stared out the window of his office, looking down at the city.

How can we be kin? You murdered my mother. Charlie's physical body would hold Grandfather's trap. He was fighting back. And he had escaped Foxx every time.

When Foxx turned to sit, Charlie thought the moment had come. *Open it, open it, open it.* But Foxx hit the intercom instead.

"Yates!"

"Yes, master?" A haunted, broken voice.

"Stop the projections. Scan the code itself. Full parallel processing. Look for any anomaly at all."

How did Foxx know?

The phone buzzed again.

"What now?" Foxx shouted.

"Mr. Foxx, Jane Virtue has landed on the roof," Evelyn said. "Shall I send her down?"

"Fine!"

"And Mr. McCallum is here to see you, with some other gentlemen."

"Then let them *in!*"

Foxx is on edge, Charlie realized.

The phone buzzed again. It was Yates's oddly monotonous voice. "Sir, the scan was negative for unauthorized code."

Charlie was elated. *Geneva's code hasn't been detected.* He wished he could tell her the good news.

McCallum entered with two men from Red Team. They carried boxes.

"This is it, sir," McCallum said. "Everything from Geneva's hiding place."

Foxx opened one. The Code Analyzer. He inspected it with intense curiosity.

Charlie watched closely. In moments, his plan would come to pass.

"Guards," Foxx said. "Leave us."

"Yes, sir."

Jane Virtue stepped into the room, radiant despite having flown halfway around the world on her publicity tour. McCallum held his polite smile, but his stomach flipped unexpectedly. What was it about her?

"Jane! You look ravishing," Foxx gushed. Ratings had gone up another 13 percent in the last few days.

"Thank you, Gramercy." Jane kissed him lightly on both cheeks, her purse over one arm. Perfect LAanges etiquette.

"You're ready for the big moment?" Foxx asked. "Everything changes tonight, my dear. I was just telling John. . . . You know John McCallum, don't you?"

"I believe we spoke on the phone," she said with a kind smile.

"Yes, ma'am." John's nerves didn't betray him. "Pleasure to meet you."

"I was about to tell John that I have just received an unexpected surprise," Foxx said. "A nasty little thing, but it doesn't matter."

"Gramercy! What is it?"

"I was about to open an email sent to me by a hacker. It contains some . . . ransom demands, for lack of a better term. I'll show you the relevant bits."

Foxx tapped the attachment. This was what Charlie had been waiting for.

PART V:
THE WAY THE
WORLD ENDS

CHAPTER 59

Crack! The air itself ripped apart, flashing as brightly as a lightning strike.

Time stopped for Charlie. One moment he was above them, omnisciently aware. The next moment, he was physically transmogrified back into a boy. Disoriented and breathless, his only thought was of Pandora's Box.

McCallum saw the flare of light reflected in Jane's glasses, saving him from the temporary blindness Jane experienced. He spun and dropped, combat-ready, sidearm out.

He couldn't believe what he saw. Curled in a ball on Gramercy Foxx's desk lay the boy he'd been pursuing: Charlie.

Foxx jumped clear, stunned by the blast. McCallum thought he would never see fear on the face of Gramercy Foxx, but for a split second, there it was. Then it was gone.

"Get him!" Foxx screamed.

Jane trembled, hands over her ears, her eyes squeezed shut.

The boy raised his head. Tucked in his arms was a puppy. Callaya growled at Foxx. The boy flexed his arms, then looked down at his legs, as if checking to be sure they were still there. He looked at McCallum and then Jane, holding the puppy tight. His eyes searched Foxx's desk as if he were missing something.

There — a carved wooden box fell to the floor beneath his feet. He reached for it weakly, but Foxx snatched the box away.

"Give me that!" the boy croaked. "It's mine!"

"Not anymore," Foxx snarled.

"It doesn't belong to you! Don't . . . don't open it!"

Callaya began to bark, but the boy did not release her.

"Get him!" Foxx shouted to McCallum.

John hesitated, but then he did as he was told. He grabbed the boy and his puppy. Charlie, held tightly by McCallum, tried to twist away. Foxx placed the box on his desk.

"Gramercy!" Jane cried. "What's happening here?"

"Calm yourself," Foxx commanded sharply. "This boy is the hacker."

"But he's a child! How did he get here?"

"He's a liar!" Charlie tried to shout. His voice gave out. "Don't . . . listen!"

"Silence!" Foxx lunged at him, striking him across the face.

The dog snapped at Foxx and tried to bite his hand. McCallum pulled Charlie and the dog away.

"Gramercy, stop!" Jane screamed over Callaya's barking and growling.

"He is trying to destroy everything we have accomplished, Jane!"

Holding the boy with one arm, McCallum kept an eye on Foxx.

"Throw the dog into the cabinet," Foxx ordered.

Still gripping the boy, McCallum pulled the writhing puppy away. He gently tossed her into the cabinet, securing the latch. The door rattled and thumped as the dog struggled to get out.

"Take the boy to his girlfriend," Foxx snapped. "They can learn about pain *together*."

Charlie looked at Jane. He tried to speak. McCallum bent to listen.

"He's saying your name, Jane."

"This meeting is over! Take him downstairs!" Foxx's voice rose.

"*My* name? Why *my* name? Please, Gramercy! Calm down!" She gently raised the boy's face to hers. "Do you know me? Or did you see me on 3D?"

"I *told* you," he whispered. "Foxx is a monster."

Despite the rasp, Jane recognized the voice. She knew it — he had been telling the truth. Foxx's actions were confirming it. "John, this is the boy I called you about — Charlie." She suddenly felt sick. "Gramercy, what is this?"

Foxx had already stopped listening. "Very well," he spat. "Free will is no longer necessary."

Every screen in the room flared to life. A pattern of dancing light and pulsing sound filled the office. McCallum and Virtue were transfixed, unable to avert their eyes, unable to close their ears.

As Foxx conducted, the two fell under the power of The Future, now complete. Their last free thoughts were of surprise — surprise at their betrayal and surprise that they were becoming victims of the very machine they had unwittingly helped to create.

❖   ❖   ❖

Charlie's head hung limply. He knew what was happening. He recognized the lights, the sound — The Future. So he played dead in McCallum's arms.

Even with his eyes closed, his mind began to drift. *Focus. You are an unmovable stone in a river. You are flooded with the Hum. Let the water flow past you. Believe.*

Charlie focused with every ounce of mental strength.

Then it all stopped. He felt McCallum's grip tighten.

"Who is your master?" Foxx demanded.

"My master's name is Callis," Jane and McCallum replied in unison. "You are our master."

Charlie didn't lift his eyes. He didn't need to. Jane and McCallum were gone — under Foxx's control now, soon to be joined by how many others?

Play dead, play dead. Charlie needed more time.

Then it hit him. Where was Pandora's Box?

He didn't have long. Foxx would take his mind, too. Or torture him.

A shadow fell across his feet. It was Foxx, inches away. *Play dead, play dead.* McCallum continued to hold him tight. Charlie would need every bit of his strength to get the job done.

Sharp fingers grabbed his cheeks and yanked his face up. He opened his eyes weakly, trying not to focus. Foxx had to believe Charlie was incapable of resistance.

Charlie could smell Foxx's stale breath.

"You have made a foolish mistake, *boy*," Foxx said with pitiless disgust. "Tell me how you know what you know, and I may let you live. What is your full name?"

Charlie allowed his eyes to focus. Then he made the only move he had.

"My box," he croaked. "In my box . . ."

"Who is your master?"

"Callis is my master," Charlie whispered weakly.

Would his little bit of acting work? *Get the box, Foxx! Get the box!*

McCallum didn't flinch. Foxx walked over to his desk.

He returned with the box and jerked Charlie's face upright again.

"Where did you get this box?" Foxx hissed.

Charlie moaned. "In . . . an old shop. In the Highlands. Near Eamsford."

"What's in it?" Foxx looked at it closely. The box was light.

"Old papers. A drawing of you. And notes," Charlie added. "From . . . Callaya."

"Impossible," Foxx spat, but he believed it. Or at least he was curious. "Who is your master?" he asked again.

"Callis is my master," Charlie said.

"What do the notes say?"

"They're about the Hum, master. That's how I learned to connect to it." Charlie feigned unconsciousness again.

Please, please underestimate me.

Foxx lightly gripped the ornately carved black lid. A box from a shop in the Highlands? It was possible — there was so much he didn't remember. But brought by a boy who then ended up in LAanges? That would be quite a coincidence. Foxx had stopped believing in coincidences years ago.

Yet the boy had used the Hum. And Callaya's notes about the Hum! Today was such an important day. But there might be something he could learn.

There was only one way to find out what was in the box. Foxx had to know. If the boy was lying, he would suffer for it.

Foxx knew something was wrong the moment he released the wooden catch. He nearly dropped the box. A swirling darkness leaped out, blocking all light. A bizarre suction pulled at his face and head. And there was the unmistakable vibration of the Hum, the very *old* Hum. . . .

Gramercy Foxx had been deceived.

CHAPTER 60

The room spun, a field of stationary stars beyond dark, swirling streaks. Pandora's Box pulled the skin of Charlie's face — it liked him, too. He wasn't prepared for its incredible strength. Luckily McCallum held him in an iron grip.

Foxx's hair streaked forward. Even his face stretched toward the box as he struggled against its power.

Then, as suddenly as it began, the tugging force waned. The spinning darkness lightened. And it all ended.

Foxx snapped the lid of the box closed.

Charlie's face no longer ached from the box's pull. Grandfather's trap had failed.

Gramercy Foxx turned his furious gaze on Charlie. His hair uncharacteristically disheveled, Foxx's face was twisted by rage. He bared his teeth in a vicious snarl. He dropped the box and struck Charlie sadistically across the face. Once. Twice. Three times. Blood flew.

McCallum and Jane Virtue did nothing.

Foxx gripped Charlie's hair. His eyes darkened. "Do you think yourself clever, boy? I will devour your mind and consume your very soul. How dare you interfere with The Future! My masterpiece!"

This was the end. *So be it*, thought Charlie. He had done what he could. Foxx had won. *First he steals hope*. The sadness was overwhelming.

"Just enough time to go see your girlfriend," Foxx hissed. "You'll find her much changed."

Crack! The dog broke through the cabinet door.

Callaya's teeth sank deep into Foxx's ankle. She refused to let go.

Foxx roared, kicking at the heavy wooden desk. A sickening thud sounded as the puppy struck the desk. She dropped limply to the ground with a whimper.

"Callaya!"

"Callaya?" Foxx exploded. That single word made everything clear. *Callaya!* How could he have missed it before? There were no papers in that box! Its purpose was clear. The pain in his ankle couldn't compare to his fury at having overlooked the obvious. "What is your name, boy?"

Charlie squirmed against McCallum's viselike arms, glaring at Foxx defiantly.

"Your name?" Foxx asked again, his voice horribly low.

"Charles."

"The Highlands, you said? Tell me, did Geneva fetch you here from across time?"

Charlie looked at Callaya, lying on the floor. He nodded. How could everything go so wrong?

Of course, Foxx thought. *But how could Geneva have known when to go, and where?* Foxx could barely remember himself. "How do you know the name Callaya?"

"You murdered her. She was my *mother*!"

"Mother?" Foxx blurted before he regained control. *Mother?* "Charles . . . Charla . . . It can't be!" He would have known, should have seen it in the boy's face. But that explained so much more. What had they done? He would find out. But for now, Foxx had all the information he needed.

The Future would not be stopped. He smiled. "John, take our friend to the computer lab. And you can take the dog, too. Make sure you put her in a cage — and lock it."

Back at his desk, Foxx held his handkerchief against his bleeding ankle. "Jane, take the box and go with them."

They obeyed. Charlie screamed uselessly. Foxx's employees had long since learned to ignore any sound behind the heavy double doors.

"Help him to be quiet."

McCallum put his strong hand over Charlie's mouth. They were on their way to the lab. No one would hear Charlie. Soon it wouldn't matter if they did.

CHAPTER 61

Jane Virtue was dreaming.

No, it's an out-of-body experience, she thought as her hands gripped the black box. She was not in control. She could hear Charlie screaming distantly, but her head wouldn't turn to look. Her legs carried her past Evelyn's office to the elevator. McCallum joined her at the elevator, arms still locked solidly around the kicking boy. Callaya was in a sack over his shoulder.

Jane's finger pressed 198. She realized she had not been herself. She had disregarded facts, satisfied to be the shining star of Gramercy Foxx's empire. But how was *that* possible? Her integrity meant *everything* to her, and she just threw it away? For what?

The elevator doors slid open.

What was happening to her? Had she gone insane? Schizophrenia could make people feel disconnected from their bodies.

The computer lab door clicked open, and her body followed McCallum in.

What she saw was horrible — a teenage girl strapped to a table, connected to electrical gear! What was Foxx doing in here?

Then she heard a voice, and she really began to fear for her sanity.

Jane. The voice was in her head. She wanted to cry.

Jane . . . can you hear me?

If she didn't answer, she wouldn't be crazy, right? Talking to yourself isn't crazy. Answering yourself *is*.

Jane, listen to me.

A man's voice. She wanted to block it out.

Jane, it's John McCallum.

John McCallum? He's right *here*! Maybe he's just talking.

Jane, don't be afraid. I can hear your thoughts. Can you hear mine? You aren't going crazy.

McCallum's lips never moved. He strapped the boy to the chair with robotic precision. Then he locked the puppy in a cage.

Jane, we're under some kind of mind control. I think this is The Future.

I can hear you, John. Is this what Foxx plans to release to billions of people?

I'm afraid so, Jane.

Foxx must have taken over part of my mind all along.

Me too, Jane.

Are there others? Was Janice Wong under this mind control? Janice had answered Jane's questions with so little emotion during Jane's interview.

Mind control or not, how could Jane have done the things she'd done in the name of Gramercy Foxx?

How could any of us?

CHAPTER 62

"Geneva," Charlie whispered, hoping she would wake up. McCallum had strapped him tightly to the chair. Now the man stood silently, controlled by The Future, as a skinny fellow typed furiously at a computer.

"Geneva!" Charlie whispered. She looked dangerously ill. "It's Charlie! Can you hear me?"

Her eyes rolled. Her cracked lips opened slowly. Foxx hadn't given her water in days.

"Chuh-ree," she croaked, barely able to say his name. "My meh-rees . . ."

"Your memories?"

She nodded almost imperceptibly. "Dehre back, Chuh-ree." Geneva's eyes rolled back in her head again, and she lost consciousness.

The door swung open. Foxx entered, limping slightly from the dog bite. His hair was slicked back, and he wore a new suit. He smiled at Charlie.

"It's so *dark* in here, Charles. Let's brighten it up! Monitors — news coverage, please." Wall-panel OLED screens blared a cacophony of the latest 3D-casts about The Future.

"She needs water."

"Electricity and water don't mix, Charles."

"She may be just a robot to you, but she still needs water."

"No, she's not *just* a robot. She has robotic *parts*. But she's a *real girl*, Charlie — every bit as real as you. Cut her, she bleeds. The whole bit. She simply . . . forgot."

"Get away from her, you *monster*." Charlie strained against the straps.

"Enough of that. Are you ready for the big show?" Foxx grinned. "Every movie theater, concert hall, sports arena, church, synagogue, and convention center — packed to maximum capacity . . . all over the world. Do you know why?"

Charlie looked away.

"What event?"

"The Future!" Charlie blurted out. It was too much. Tears trickled down his cheeks.

"That's right. The *Future!*" Foxx reveled in it. "And *you* were here for one reason, weren't you? What reason was that?"

"To stop you!" Tears flowed now.

"Yes," Foxx said. "And you *failed*, didn't you?"

Charlie couldn't stop crying.

"Answer me!"

"Yes." Charlie was utterly broken. "I failed."

"You *failed*."

Foxx mussed Charlie's hair, adding insult to injury. "That wasn't so hard, was it? I think this is the part where I'm supposed to ask you to join me. You beg me to spare your life —"

"Never!"

"I didn't offer, kid," Foxx said sharply. "That's how the story goes in the movies. Not here. This is *my* game. Check. Mate.

"Jane!" Foxx said. "Get to makeup. And, dear, act normal, won't you?" Jane adjusted her suit jacket and strode out of the room wearing a charming smile.

Charlie was powerless. Hacking into The Future code had failed. Pandora's Box had failed.

The box was probably the only way to stop Foxx, outside of killing him. It was just across the room, but it may as well have been on the moon. Besides, the box was a dud.

Foxx had murdered Charlie's mother, and Charlie would never avenge her death. His best friend lay dying. He had never had a real friend before. And now he couldn't even bring her a sip of water. Callaya had been locked up and would either be killed or taken away.

The Future was very bleak indeed.

CHAPTER 63

"Miss Virtue, Miss Virtue!" Claudia, the makeup assistant, shouted down the long hallway. "We're seven minutes behind schedule!"

"Then you'd better hurry!" Jane heard herself say. She'd turned into a nightmare.

It was time for the final half-hour presentation. Thirty minutes of . . . of what?

Propaganda.

Keep people interested long enough to turn them into zombies.

Jane's body sat silently in the chair, but inside she desperately wanted to tell Claudia to run and save herself. *Do not watch The Future!*

"Our little friend, Geneva, can turn electricity into the Hum," Foxx said. "She doesn't know that, of course. After all, the Hum is just another form of energy.

"I *gave* her that ability. She was to take me time traveling. But it didn't work out."

"Neither did your dog," Charlie said, hoping to hit a nerve.

"A flawed concept," Foxx snapped. "Too complicated to —"

"It's simple, actually," Charlie interrupted. "Want to know what went wrong?"

"Do tell," Foxx said, sneering.

"She doesn't *like* you."

"Watch your mouth, boy," Foxx said, deadly quiet.

"The Hum likes *her*. Maybe because her name is Callaya."

Foxx ignored him. "Well, the Hum just isn't what it used to be. It turns out all those believers that I killed were important. If no one believes, it just doesn't work.

"Do you know why the Hum involves blood?" Foxx asked. "DNA. The Future is essentially digital DNA, and the Hum *loves* it. It spreads on its own, from person to person, without electricity or computers at all. Under my control, people will generate Hum energy the way a power plant generates electricity. And I will *use* that energy."

Charlie shook his head. "You don't understand the Hum at all, do you? No wonder my mother was so much better."

"How dare you!" Foxx hissed. "*The Hum will return!* And it will be *mine*." He collected himself. "The Future launches in fifteen minutes. By sunset tomorrow, the entire world will be under my direct control. This is the dawn of a new era — the Hum and technology . . . coexisting."

CHAPTER 64

McCallum stiffly followed Foxx to the studio. His mind screamed to grab the monster by the neck and choke the life out of him. But he was a prisoner in his own skin.

Jane was on the air, broadcasting to billions. Contest winners filled the studio audience. Fourteen million people had entered for fifty available slots to see The Future unveiled by Gramercy Foxx — live and in the flesh. Jane's body chatted away to the audience and the cameras while her mind shouted for everyone to run away. But only John McCallum could hear her.

Five minutes to The Future.

Gramercy Foxx entered. McCallum followed. He was the security detail.

Now Jane and Foxx would discuss The Future, as cameras blasted it to a worldwide audience.

"Some claim you're a savior who has come to bring peace to humankind," Jane read from the prompter.

"Well, Jane," Foxx said, his public charm on full display, "I certainly don't claim that. We're talking about a global shift. We've seen them before. Fire enabled mankind to survive the elements, while agriculture enabled us to grow food and build societies. I'm no savior. I'm just a simple man who discovered the next step."

"These are the final moments. Over nine *billion* people are watching right now, Mr. Foxx, in every language on the planet. Do you have anything else you'd like to say to us before The Future is unveiled?"

Foxx grinned, barely able to hold back a burst of laughter. His eyes danced, a hint of mania shining through. He had never put on such a convincing act in his life.

"Dictators rise and fall, economies crash and boom. But underneath it all, the desire for brotherhood has been suppressed by greed. We are about to move past that to a new era of harmony."

"Thank you for sharing with us, Mr. Foxx," Jane said, turning to the camera. "I believe I speak for everyone watching when I say . . . Mr. Gramercy Foxx, will you show us all The Future?" The studio audience cheered and clapped loudly.

The cameras pulled away, revealing the video walls behind them.

Foxx drew up to his full, proud height and smiled. It was too late now — no one could stop him.

Foxx raised his arms. The crowd cheered. "Ladies and gentlemen of the world! The Future . . . is *NOW*!"

And with that, life on planet Earth changed forever.

CHAPTER 65

The Future worked. It did precisely what Foxx promised — it united people.

Jane Virtue knew first. The studio audience succumbed quickly. Their excited anticipation gave way to rapt awe. Instead of control, as with Virtue and McCallum, Foxx started spreading The Future with a flood of euphoria for the physical body and consciousness. That would give him the time he needed.

The brilliant code Geneva had slipped into The Future enhanced their feeling of unity, perforating the firewall that would have silenced them, allowing communication.

Completely unaware, Foxx slipped back upstairs.

"Yates!" Foxx shouted as he burst into the machine room. "Status!"

Screens of data sprang up. The code was spreading like digital wildfire. The Future was the ultimate Trojan horse — everyone wanted it.

The code reported back on every infected system and person. Infection rates and numbers of confirmed zombies displayed on a screen showing locations — free green clusters turned zombie red. It had taken only twelve minutes for LAanges to go completely red.

Screens also showed the multitudes of rapt faces in large public venues.

"Excellent," Foxx said, watching his creation come to life on screen after screen. Satisfied, he closed his eyes to tap into the Hum flow and guide The Future.

McCallum couldn't see Jane anymore, much less hear her — the noise of people's thought was pure chaos. The original feelings of bliss were turning to confusion. What was happening?

Jane! Jane! No response.

He was a man of action, but what could he do when he had no power to move?

His mind had been able to talk with Jane; maybe he could talk to the others.

My name is John McCallum. He directed his thought at the closest man. If he had to reach each confused person one by one, then he would try that. What choice did he have?

My name is John McCallum. Can you hear me? My name is John McCallum.

Foxx hovered at the edge of metaphysical consciousness. He focused the flow. The Future was spreading faster and faster. Most of the coast was his, and inland, the municipalities were turning. Nations across the oceans were changing from green to red, following the fiber-optic lines that crossed the vast seas.

He turned to the two who had tried to stop him. Geneva's dry eyes were stuck open, and her parched tongue adhered to the roof of her mouth. Charlie, bound to the chair, sat still with his eyes closed. He was trying to disappear.

"My, you do have lots of energy. Good. I want to harness that," Foxx said.

Charlie opened his eyes. "Let her go. You're killing her."

"Oh, I'll get around to that. You should have stayed home, Charles."

"What you're doing is against nature."

"Against nature? This *is* nature! Survival of the fittest — *I'm* the fittest!"

"You're taking away freedom!"

"Freedom has been an illusion since the invention of the credit card! People are already slaves to capitalism and consumerism. Buy, buy, buy! Work your entire lives away and *love* it! For *garbage*."

"People should choose!"

"They already have."

Foxx fired up a monitor, and The Future began its assault on Charlie.

"I don't need to justify anything. I know the difference between good and evil. It simply doesn't apply to survival. If a starving man steals, is that evil? If a man kills to defend himself, is that evil? This is for the greater good."

He's trying to control me, too, Charlie realized. The eternal, cosmic patterns on the screen made Charlie relax. Slowly he was giving in.

Suddenly a powerful rush of the Hum began to flow up, into Charlie's feet. Instead of being drained, Charlie began to feel more and more energy, as if his batteries were being recharged. Foxx was directing the Hum energy into him.

"Who is your master?" Foxx said.

"Callis," Charlie heard himself say. "You are my master."

"Now you will do as I say."

Charlie held perfectly still.

"This is going to work!" Foxx was gleeful. "With you in my power, I'll be able to break through again. I will finally be able to go *home*."

CHAPTER 66

Something shifted. McCallum's communication with the people was no longer a struggle — they heard him, and they took courage. He was a natural leader with enormous strength of character.

He had spoken his name, and people listened. The confusion faded. Recognition sparked, and it spread. What he experienced next he would never understand. Slowly at first, then all at once, a wave of energy rose inside of him.

Charlie could feel McCallum, too. He sensed the power of the man's belief, and he understood the most important thought of all. John McCallum was right — humanity could bond together and rise up.

Believe . . .

Freedom was possible. McCallum *knew* they would be free and Foxx would fail. Freedom was too deeply ingrained in the human psyche, human DNA. *People are wired to be connected — to care about one another.* Humanity would be . . .

Free.

One word echoed in his mind and out through his now

connected mind, spreading across the masses as quickly as The Future had spread:

Believe . . .

Believe . . .

Believe . . .

CHAPTER 67

Charlie was blinded by a brilliant flash of light.

Countless souls lay flattened by a detonation rippling outward. But it wasn't destruction. It was creation. Belief spread like the blast of a hydrogen bomb. The ripple — the concussion wave — spread toward him at the speed of thought. It struck Charlie, and he recognized it.

Believe . . . Believe . . . Believe . . .

Suddenly the sensation of helplessness passed away, and Charlie realized he once again controlled his body. What had changed?

Tremendous power surged around him — the Hum. He hadn't felt Hum energy this powerful since he left his own time. No, he'd never felt it!

But Foxx would feel it, too.

"No!" Foxx shrieked. "What's happening?" The map was turning from red back to green, one spot at a time.

Callaya felt it, too. Charlie watched her rip the door of her cage open.

Suddenly Charlie knew he could do the same. He focused on the flood of Hum energy. With a few simple notes he easily broke the straps holding him.

Was The Future vanishing?

Foxx screamed.

This was the moment to strike. Charlie grabbed Callaya and thrust an arm toward Foxx, palm out.

The unexpected force of energy that exploded from Charlie's hand knocked Foxx to the ground. The lights dimmed.

Charlie let out a deep breath. He dragged himself to his feet. Foxx lay still. Pandora's Box was on the table.

"Geneva?"

No response. If it weren't for her shallow, panting breath, Charlie would have thought she was dead. He disconnected the electrical lines and grabbed a bottle of water. He sprinkled some into her mouth and a little on her face. He didn't want to make her sick. He waited, and then he did it again. Callaya, up on the table, licked Geneva's ear.

Her eyes rolled slightly. A sign of life, at least. Relief washed over Charlie for the first time since she'd been kidnapped.

"Geneva, we did it."

"I wouldn't go that far," a singsong voice said.

Charlie spun.

Foxx wasted no time. A bolt of energy hit Charlie, and he collapsed in agony. Pandora's Box skittered across the floor.

"Never turn your back on your enemies," Foxx taunted.

Despite the pain, Charlie grabbed Callaya and thrust his palm forward again.

The new blast of energy ricocheted harmlessly off of Foxx and into a rack of computer gear. It exploded in a burst of sparks and debris.

Charlie looked around, panicked. He reached for Pandora's Box.

But why would it work now?

There was no other choice. Charlie flipped the latch.

Pandora's Box was open.

Charlie's entire world went dark.

The spinning blackness returned, enveloping him along with Foxx. The box was so strong now that Charlie felt his flesh being pulled. His entire being stretched and compressed. It sucked him in with a power he'd never felt before.

Foxx could no more resist Pandora's pull than Charlie had. The box trapped both Foxx and Charlie in the blink of an eye.

CHAPTER 68

Charlie floated in limbo. Surely he must be dead. Then he remembered. *I'm a prisoner in Pandora's Box. But what about Foxx?*

He tried to see in the darkness. The world rotated around him.

A point of light in the distance grew, and the light became Foxx. Not the Gramercy Foxx Charlie had seen in the flesh, but Foxx as he should have appeared — an incredibly old man, if you could even call him that.

Foxx had cheated time, living impossibly long in a place that was not his own. Inside Pandora's Box, his toothless mouth gaped open in a silent moan, mirroring the blackness around them. The rattling whisper of the near-dead man seeped directly into Charlie's mind. *You have made a terrible mistake, boy. Before I escape from this child's attempt at a prison, I will show you what it is to have your soul eaten.* Charlie tried to run, but his efforts were fruitless. Foxx's toothless mouth opened even wider, and Charlie felt a tug at his mind.

What did you do to my mother? It was his final question, the only thing left to say. He repeated it over and over. The darkness of Foxx's power closed in.

But suddenly a light in the darkness descended from above. Foxx looked up to the source of the interruption. He fell back.

Release my son.

Her son? Charlie raised his eyes to the light. Kindness poured down into him, filling him with love and awe.

Callaya? Foxx rasped. *This cannot be!*

But it is, brother, it is.

You're too late. Foxx pounded Charlie's mind, threatening to split into it from sheer force.

Callis, I should strike you down and cast you into oblivion. But Charles will not learn vengeance from me. I have spent a hundred lifetimes learning to forgive you.

Foxx raged. *I understand more than you know! How dare you condescend —*

SILENCE!

Charlie sensed that her power was great.

The Hum is not a tool. It is a source of beauty, the center of all living things. It thrives on belief — on love. You awakened them, brought them together. Humanity broke free, Callis. The Hum thrives again. Now go!

The old man receded in the distance. Instantly he was light-years away.

It's really you? Charlie asked without speaking.

The body is only a shell. The light — the Hum — comes from within.

Are you the Hum?

We all are. You know that.

What did Callis do to you? And why?

None of that matters. Beyond the physicality of space and time, things are very different. You can hear me because we are in this place.

Mother . . . Charlie had wanted to say that for so long. He choked up.

There is more at stake here than my brother's sad attempt to create a world of slaves, Charles. He could never have succeeded — humankind cannot be enslaved. The spirit is too strong.

They said you were dead.

We all exist beyond space and time. Do you understand?

He didn't.

I'm always nearby, Charles. Remember that. You may not see me or hear me, but I'm in a world that is closer than your own skin.

Can I come back here to see you again? he asked.

No. You must leave. I'm so sorry, my love, but time has run out.

A point of light quickly grew into the form of Callis again — his twisted face a wreck of silent, immobile fury.

Callis, Callaya said, *I am releasing my son from this prison. You will stay.*

Hear me, I beg, Callis cried desperately. *Everything I have done has been out of —*

Selfishness! she interrupted. *Now you will suffer the consequences!*

Callis shivered. Once again he shrank back into a point of light.

I'm so proud of you, Charles, she said. *You have made strong choices. We will both be removed from this place now. Remember that I love you. Believe* . . .

Charlie felt the pulling blackness begin to swirl around him again. He was being released from Pandora's Box. . . .

CHAPTER 69

Not a moment had passed.

Callaya was curled beside Geneva, and Lawrence Yates was still unconscious. Pandora's Box truly existed outside of space and time.

Charlie spun around, panicked that the box would be gone. Gramercy Foxx could be behind him, preparing another attack. Had he imagined everything?

No. Foxx had disappeared. The charcoal-black box sat in his place. Locked inside, he couldn't hurt anyone now.

Was there an entire universe inside Pandora's Box? All that blackness — it had seemed infinite. And how had his mother intervened? Charlie was too exhausted to understand. He picked up the box. It *was* heavier. Grandfather was right.

His mother! Charlie would ask Grandfather when he returned.

But what now?

He ran to Geneva. She looked up at him wearily when he held her hand. "Charlie?"

"I'm here."

"Did you do it?" She tried to look around the destroyed room.

The door burst open. John McCallum dashed in, gun raised. His flashlight flared in the dim emergency lighting.

"Don't shoot!"

"Kids, are you in here? I'm not gonna hurt you!"

Jane Virtue ran into the room at the sound of Charlie's voice. "Charlie?" She grabbed him by the shoulders. "Are you OK?"

"I am," he said. "But Geneva . . ."

"I'm so sorry. Foxx was . . . he made us . . ."

"Where *is* Foxx?" McCallum asked, tending to Geneva and releasing her from the restraints.

"He's in there," Charlie said, pointing at Pandora's Box.

"Gramercy Foxx is *in* here?" McCallum asked, picking it up.

"Don't open it!"

"I won't, but we'll need a safe place to put it."

"No! I'm going home. And I'm taking it with me," Charlie insisted. "My grandfather will know what to do with it."

"Sir!" Two members of the security team dashed in. "The audience is evacuating down the emergency stairs, as ordered."

"Any problems?"

"None. They're helping one another."

McCallum nodded.

"Permission to speak freely, sir?" McCallum allowed it. The two Reds stumbled over each other's words.

"What you did for us . . ."

"The people back there, they were all talking about it . . ."

"I don't understand what happened, but . . ."

"You saved us, sir."

"You brought us out of it, sir."

"That flash of light! That was you . . ."

"Wasn't it?"

245

McCallum thought about it all. What *had* happened? They had been under Foxx's control. People had *heard* him. The sense of community had been so strong. Had there been a revolution? Then the explosion, the flash of light. It had all happened so fast. He didn't know what to make of it, but he *had* been at the center of it.

"I don't know," McCallum said with great hesitation. "I wasn't alone."

The Hum, Charlie thought. *A man like Foxx could never understand it.*

Charlie squeezed Geneva's hand tightly.

"Blue Bird, come in," McCallum said into the radio. "Yeah, McCallum here. . . . Yes, *that* McCallum. Thank you. Yeah, OK. I love you, too. Look, pick us up on the TerraThinc pad. I know it's high. Are you OK to fly? OK, good. Just get there. Four of us coming out."

Charlie helped get Geneva down from Foxx's table. She rolled her nano-skin back down over her robotic hands like a pair of gloves.

"You did it, didn't you, Charlie?" she asked weakly.

"*We* did it."

CHAPTER 70

"You're sure you don't want to come with me?" Charlie asked over his shoulder from the passenger seat of McCallum's Command Vehicle.

"I have things to check out, other times to explore," Geneva said from the back. "Honestly, the memories that have returned have only raised more questions."

A week had passed since the release of The Future. Geneva had been searching for answers. She had subjected herself to numerous scans to reveal her robotic parts. But it didn't answer her most fundamental question — who *was* she? Every answer yielded another question. She planned to find the truth, and hopefully her identity.

"Well, I can't force you, but I hope you'll visit," Charlie said with a smile. He turned to John McCallum, in the driver's seat. "You'll take care of everything, won't you?"

"I'll do my best," McCallum said. "Jane and I have a lot of work to do. People are looking to us for guidance — the highest levels of government. They've got us on a plane later today. We may even have to go speak to the chancellor himself. I don't want to know where, or *when*, you're going," he said firmly. "The government doesn't know the truth about either of you, and they won't learn it from me."

247

The search for Gramercy Foxx had become a worldwide manhunt. People wanted an explanation.

Foxx had been correct that The Future had brought unity to the planet. But not the way he intended it to happen, through mind control and slavery. Instead, a sense of community and cooperation had shifted the world. Once the spokesperson for Gramercy Foxx, Jane Virtue was now the most prominent human-rights activist on the planet.

This morning was the first time the police had managed to get the streets back to anything resembling normal. This was McCallum's first opportunity to get Charlie and Geneva away.

"You're a very brave young man. Even with your . . . the . . . supernatural stuff," McCallum said, searching for the words, "you've shown real courage."

Charlie felt a lump in his throat. He didn't know what to say.

"Best of luck, Charlie," McCallum said warmly. "And to you, too, Geneva."

Charlie climbed out of the truck into the street, carrying Callaya. He pulled his pack tighter onto his back. Geneva slipped out after. McCallum's team had cordoned off a block to keep the public away from one particular open manhole. *Smasher,* Charlie thought. The Hum was so strong now.

He looked over his shoulder and waved back at McCallum. Geneva stood next to Charlie, ready to go. Charlie would miss her, but she could take care of herself. He and Grandfather needed to leave their mountain. It had become too dangerous.

Charlie had a long story to tell. And he had some questions, too.

"I thought you were human all along," Charlie said.

"Did you?" Geneva asked, amused.

"Yeah, I only make friends with humans. It's kind of a rule I have." They smiled at each other. Their adventure had come to an end.

"Well, you said you went back on your own. Show me what you can do. You ready to smash some atoms?"

Charlie closed his eyes. The Hum poured into his feet so powerfully that the portal opened effortlessly. He looked over at her.

"Not bad for a twelve-year-old." She smirked.

"Thirteen," he corrected. "My birthday was last week."

"What? Happy birthday! Why didn't you say anything?"

"There was a lot going on that day. You'll be OK?"

"Of course. Besides, I know where to find help."

"Yeah, me too," he said with a smile.

The swirling blue portal awaited them.

"After you," Geneva said.

Charlie was ready to go home.

Home. Grandfather and the cottage.

"Geneva, what about the Interrogator?"

"The future is relative, Charlie," she said. "*Your* future, that is. Besides, I'm pretty sure you can handle whatever comes."

"Right." He reminded himself of what he had just accomplished. His grandfather had changed, too. Charlie was pretty sure the days of conflict and fear were over.

He closed his eyes, straightened his pack, and held his puppy tightly in his arms. He stepped in.

The familiar splash and disorientation of the blue time water preceded Charlie's first deep breath. Geneva appeared next to him, loose hair flowing all around her in an angelic aura.

The two friends clasped hands one last time. *Later, friend.* Geneva's voice echoed in his mind as she shot him a mischievous, knowing smile. Then she darted away, propelled by rippling energy waves.

Charlie was looking forward to his little bed. And a simple life again. He'd had enough adventure for now. Maybe Grandfather would make him a cup of his favorite tea, sweetened with honey.

Friend.

He headed home.

ACKNOWLEDGMENTS

First and foremost, I would like to thank Audrey, my confidant, love, and laugh-mate. She read the first draft, generously lied to me and said it was good, and then continued to put up with me through every stressful draft that followed.

I am grateful to my agent, Deborah Warren, and her inimitable husband, Phil.

Thanks to Cameron Malin with the FBI for his enthusiastic technical review, and to Jim Davidson for the introduction.

Thank you, Christine Cuddy, for legal counsel, and Lisa Yee and Michael Reisman for writer's counsel — you helped this book noob learn the ropes.

And thank you to my many readers for helping me to find the ghosts in the machine — Jessica, Alex, Jay, Brandon, Nate, Bob, Kaitlin, Declan, Laura, Paul, Shawn, Kerry, Noam, and Tom. I mentioned Audrey already, right?

A very special thanks to the assistant editorial crew at Scholastic — Sara Waltuck and Grace Kendall.

And the biggest thanks of all go to my über-editor, Bonnie Verburg, without whom this would never even have begun. Bonnie, thank you so much for getting a virus on your computer, and even more for asking me if I'd ever thought about writing a children's book.